"I had reasons

Angela spun arou[n]... in his tracks. "I wouldn't know, now, would I?" She poked a finger at his chest. "Because you didn't bother to tell me what they were, or even that you were leaving. I had to find out from your roommate, *after* you were long gone." She smacked her palm flat against his chest. "You'd think any kind of man would have the decency to tell his girlfriend he was skipping town, quitting college and joining the navy. But then, you weren't even decen—"

Buck grabbed her arms and yanked her against him, crushing her lips with a bruising kiss. He'd never wanted to leave her, would rather have slit his own throat than hurt her. And now, seeing her in front of him, her eyes alight with fury, her cheeks blooming with righteous indignation, he couldn't resist.

This was the woman he'd never been able to forget.

THREE COURAGEOUS WORDS

New York Times **Bestselling Author**

ELLE JAMES

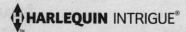
HARLEQUIN INTRIGUE®

To my husband, who swears he doesn't have a creative bone in his body, for giving me the idea to have a villain warlord who conscripts young boys into his terrorist army. When I ask my husband for help brainstorming, I see the fear in his eyes. This time, he came through!

ISBN-13: 978-1-335-52653-3

Three Courageous Words

Copyright © 2018 by Mary Jernigan

Recycling programs for this product may not exist in your area.

Printed in U.S.A.

Elle James, a *New York Times* bestselling author, started writing when her sister challenged her to write a romance novel. She has managed a full-time job and raised three wonderful children, and she and her husband even tried ranching exotic birds (ostriches, emus and rheas). Ask her, and she'll tell you what it's like to go toe-to-toe with an angry 350-pound bird! Elle loves to hear from fans at ellejames@earthlink.net or ellejames.com.

Books by Elle James

Harlequin Intrigue

Mission: Six

One Intrepid SEAL
Two Dauntless Hearts
Three Courageous Words

Ballistic Cowboys

Hot Combat
Hot Target
Hot Zone
Hot Velocity

SEAL of My Own

Navy SEAL Survival
Navy SEAL Captive
Navy SEAL to Die For
Navy SEAL Six Pack

Visit the Author Profile page at Harlequin.com.

CAST OF CHARACTERS

"Buck" Graham Bucker—US Navy SEAL, team medic. Went to medical school but didn't finish. Joined the navy, became a SEAL, and left Chicago and his dangerous past behind.

Dr. Angela Vega—Provides medical care for people in a South Sudanese refugee camp as part of Doctors Without Borders. Fell in love with a fellow medical student and was crushed when he left medical school and her without a word. Sworn off falling in love again.

General Ibrahim Koku—Sudanese warlord responsible for diverting aid packages to refugee camps and conscripting children into his terrorist army.

Abu Hanafi—South Sudanese village elder.

Mustafa—Boy who escaped Koku's training camp to return home.

Marly Simpson—Bush pilot in Africa. Her father was a bush pilot and taught her to fly. Her mother teaches children in the poor villages of Africa.

Talia Montclair—Owner/operator of the All Things Wild Resort in Kenya.

"Diesel" Dalton Samuel Landon—US Navy SEAL. Gunner and team lead.

"Pitbull" Percy Taylor—US Navy SEAL, tough guy who doesn't date much. Raised by a taciturn US Marines father. Lives by the rules and structure. SOC-R boat captain.

"Harm" Harmon Payne—US Navy SEAL. For a big guy, he's light on his feet and fast. Good at silent entry into buildings.

"Big Jake" Jake Schuler—US Navy SEAL, demolitions expert. Good at fine finger work.

"T-Mac" Trace McGuire—US Navy SEAL, communications man, equipment expert.

Chapter One

"R&R is over, team." Navy SEAL Corpsman Graham "Buck" Buckner clapped his hands together as he walked across the fourth floor of the bombed-out apartment building in Bentiu, South Sudan. "It's time to do what we do best."

"Yeah, Buck." Diesel lay prone, staring through the sight of his M4A1 rifle with the SOPMOD upgrade. "And what's that? Lying around in the heat, waiting for something to happen?"

"Men, we're here on an important mission." Buck grinned. "So what if it's hotter than Hades outside and we haven't had a breeze in over a week? We're here to get our man. Let's do this."

"Shut up, Buck," T-Mac said. "Nothing's stirred in this godforsaken town since we got here."

"That doesn't mean it won't. The intel guys said we'd find Koku here. My gut tells me it won't be long before something happens."

"Your gut is telling you that you're hungry." Pitbull tossed a packet of meals ready to eat at Buck. "Feed your gut."

Buck ducked, letting the MRE packet fall to the floor, unheeded. "Seriously, we've been in worse situations where we all almost died. This isn't that bad."

"At least our enemies weren't boring us to death," Pitbull said. He pulled a photograph from his pocket and stared down at it. "We could have spent two more days at the All Things Wild Resort, enjoying our last little bit of rest and relaxation." He sighed. "I wonder if Marly's packing her apartment in Nairobi right now. I'd like to have been there to help her."

Harm snorted. "You're just afraid she'll say, *What the hell was I thinking, falling for a navy SEAL?* She might change her mind and stay in Africa."

Pitbull's lips twisted. "Yeah. I guess I am afraid of that. Why would she give up her life here in Africa to be with me?"

"Yeah, who'd want to give up a life in Africa?" T-Mac quipped. "It's such a bowl of cherries, what with pirates, warlords and tribal wars everywhere you turn. Think of the excitement she'll be missing."

"And why wouldn't she want to be with you?" Diesel asked. "Some women like ugly mugs like yours."

"Hey, you found a woman here," Pitbull reminded him. "And you're no Mr. *GQ* yourself."

"Ha! Wait until she realizes he snores like a freight train," Big Jake murmured from his position on the other side of the room, holding a pair of binoculars to his eyes. "You and Diesel are just mad you didn't get to spend more time with your women—now that you *have* women." He glanced back at them. "Get over it. Like Buck said, we have a job to do. Let's do it."

Buck crossed to where Big Jake leaned his elbows on the rubble that had once been a wall. "Anything?" he asked, staring out at the buildings they'd been surveilling since they'd arrived.

"Not much," Big Jake said. "Our old man with the mule cart is passing in front of the compound now. You could set the clock by that man. Same time every day."

"I'll take watch for now," Buck offered.

"Good. My eyes are crossing." Big Jake handed the binoculars to Buck. "If you're not going to eat those MREs, I will."

"Knock yourself out." Buck rubbed a hand over his flat abs. "My belly isn't over the brisket with au gratin potatoes I had for breakfast."

"We tried to warn you about them," Harm said.

Buck couldn't deny it. Harm had told him it would mess him up. His stomach was still burbling four hours later. "Yeah, well, I'll listen next time." He lifted the binoculars to his eyes and focused on the structure on the other side of the bombed-out marketplace.

The intel guys had identified the compound as one that General Ibrahim Koku frequented—a local government facility where he had friends conspiring with him to make life hell for the people of Sudan and South Sudan.

The general was a defector from the South Sudan Army and the self-appointed leader of the Sudanese People's Resistance Army, which had been terrorizing South Sudan for the past fourteen months, killing entire populations of villages and conscripting children to be part of his army. As if that wasn't bad enough, he was also the primary reason US aid wasn't getting to the starving people in refugee camps in Sudan's Darfur region, or anywhere else, for that matter. He'd stolen food, medical supplies and even the vehicles transporting them.

And when US money was being thrown away on aid, the American government sent in their boys to fix it. So, instead of enjoying a full week off for much-needed rest and relaxation, the SEAL team had been called back to duty from their Kenyan safari vacation two days early. And for what? To sit in the heat of the sub-Saharan desert and roast like pigs on a spit.

They didn't know when the general would show up, just that their mission was to take him out when he did.

Buck expanded his view to take in more of the surrounding area. A couple blocks to the south, a crowd of women gathered, growing in number as the woman in the center raised her fist to the sky, probably shouting something. From the distance, Buck couldn't hear what was being said, but the crowd responded, chanting something he couldn't understand. As one, the crowd turned and marched down the middle of the street, headed north on the same boulevard where the general's compound stood.

In the opposite direction, a number of blocks away, a motorcade of black SUVs sped south, on a collision course with the women staging a protest.

"Heads up," Buck said to his teammates. "Things are about to get interesting. Motorcade coming from the north."

Diesel shifted his body and weapon. "Got the vehicles in my sights."

"And what looks like a riot coming from the south," Buck added.

"A riot?" Harm asked and hurried to where Buck stood to see for himself.

Big Jake, T-Mac and Pitbull took up positions against the crumbling walls.

"Holy crap, if those women are on a mission to protest our favorite general, they're going to be slaughtered."

"What can we do?" Buck asked.

"Nothing," Big Jake said. "We're not here to stop them from protesting. We're here to take out Koku."

Buck glanced toward the oncoming motorcade. "Yeah, but—"

"No buts," Big Jake said. "We're here to stop Koku's reign of terror. The end. No side trips to the mall, no flirting with the local girls."

Buck lifted the binoculars again and focused on the woman leading the march. Unlike the others, who were dressed in brightly colored head scarves and dresses, the woman's head was bare. She had dark hair, dark eyes and much lighter skin than the other women marching. And she wore faded blue jeans and a white T-shirt with a red design and black lettering. "Guys, is that woman wearing a Doctors Without Borders T-shirt?" He handed the binoculars to Harm.

"Damn. She is," Harm said. "And she's not Sudanese."

"What the hell is she doing?" T-Mac asked.

"I don't know, but I'm going to get closer before all hell breaks loose," Buck said.

"Stand down, Buck," Big Jake said.

"If that woman is American, she'll be worse than

killed," Buck said. "Let me get close enough to find out. If she's American, I'll—"

"You'll what?" Big Jake shook his head. "You can't jeopardize this mission because some do-gooder has decided to march against a murdering terrorist."

"I can't do nothing." Buck lifted the binoculars again. Something about the woman seemed familiar. Maybe it was the way she walked or flipped her hair back over her shoulder, but whatever it was brought back memories he'd thought long forgotten. "I'll get her out of the way before the motorcade gets there."

Big Jake's eyes narrowed. "You can't do anything to make us miss this opportunity to take down Koku."

Buck stood and held up his hand as if swearing in court. "I promise."

Big Jake jerked his head to the side. "Go. But don't do anything stupid, and don't give yourself away. We've got your back, but don't force us to expose our position. There's too much riding on this mission's success."

Buck pulled on one of the long white robes called a dishdasha, worn by Sudanese men, and settled a white turban on his head as he ran for the stairs leading to the ground. He only had a couple minutes to get to the marching women and decide what to do before the motorcade arrived.

Keeping to the shadows, he ran along the walls of the bombed-out building between their hideout and the compound. If he were spotted, his white skin would stand out, even though most of it was covered. His tanned face and hands were not nearly dark enough to match the skin of the Sudanese men.

As he arrived near the street where the women were marching, the motorcade of black vehicles rolled into sight.

Buck cursed. If he made any kind of move to get out in front of the mob of women, he'd be picked off immediately.

Instead, he waited in the shadows for the leader of the march to pass. As she neared, a knot formed in his gut next to the one created by the MREs.

He knew her. Buck knew the woman leading the march. At least, he'd known her back in Chicago, what seemed like a million years ago.

How in the hell did she get here, half a world away from where he'd first met her?

Now more than ever, he had to get to her, to pull her out of harm's way before the motorcade reached them.

Women in brightly colored clothing passed him,

filling the streets, all chanting. Some were carrying signs Buck couldn't read.

Ducking low, Buck melted into the crowd, working his way to the front where the woman led the march, yelling loud and clear in that voice he'd recognize anywhere.

When there were only two people between them, he made his move. He dashed up behind her, spun her around and threw her over his shoulder, then ran back through the women in the crowd. He did it so quickly, the women didn't realize what was going on until he had her back by the building, in the shadows, yelling at him.

He shot a glance over his shoulder at the women who'd been marching. They'd stopped shouting and were scattering in all directions as the black vehicles rolled up to the compound.

"Put me down!" Buck's captive said. She pounded his back and kicked her legs, squirming so wildly he all but dropped her on her feet.

As soon as she had her legs under her, she cocked her arm and smacked him upside the head.

She hit him hard enough to make his ears ring.

With the motorcade so close to where they stood, Buck didn't have time to explain. He spun her around, her back to his front, clamped a hand over her mouth and dragged her deeper in the shadows.

She fought, kicking, scratching and finally biting his hand so hard she almost drew blood.

"Damn it, Angela! It's me," he whispered. "Graham."

DR. ANGELA VEGA STILLED. Her pounding heart stopped for a fraction of a second before racing ahead, for an entirely different reason than fear. "Let go of me," she demanded.

"Only if you promise not to run," he said in that deep voice she remembered all too well.

She hesitated a moment, her pulse pounding, and then said, "I promise."

Her captor released her.

Angela spun to face the man who'd turned her world upside down years ago, while she'd been in medical school. So many questions ran through her head, like what was he doing here? And why was he dressed like a Sudanese man? But she had more immediate issues. "Why did you stop me?" She spun toward the road he'd yanked her off. "I was leading those women in protest. I need to be out there."

His lips thinned. "They scattered. You won't get them back together any time soon."

"Damn it, Graham. They need food and medicine. We needed our voices to be heard by the local government officials."

"Not there, you don't." He gripped her hand in his. "Come on, we have to get out of here, ASAP."

"I'm not going anywhere with you. I work with those women. They need our assistance. Their entire families need help. And the local government is working with Koku, a bastard of a warlord, stealing the aid packages that are supposed to be going to the refugee camps."

"And you think a protest is going to make a difference?" Buck shook his head.

"We had to do something," Angela said. "The local government wasn't helping."

"I'm not here to argue with you. I'm just telling you that you're in danger."

She jerked her hand free of his and squared off with him, her shoulders back, her chin held high. "We knew that when we started. It was a risk we were all willing to take."

"Yeah, well, the only way to reason with a man like Koku is with force."

"We were protesting the local government, not Koku," Angela insisted.

"Since they're in cahoots with him, it's the same thing." He narrowed his eyes and took a threatening step toward her. "Now, are you coming with me peacefully, or am I going to have to carry you out of here?"

Angela backed up a step, then another. "I don't have to go with you. I have to get back to my practice."

"You're not going anywhere without me until we know what's happening. And the longer we stand here arguing, the greater chance there is of one of Koku's men finding us and settling our argument with bullets." He lunged toward her, bending as if to scoop her up.

"Hold it right there, buddy," she said. "You don't have to carry me like a Neanderthal."

Sounds of gunfire erupted.

Angela ducked, her heart pounding. Maybe he was right. Now wasn't the time to argue. "Fine. I'll go with you. For the time being..."

Graham grabbed her hand and ran, leading her away from the street and into the shadows of a crumbling wall. They followed the wall until they came to the back of the building, which was no more than a pile of rubble.

"Where are we going?" she asked. "And what the hell is happening back there?"

He nodded toward the damaged apartment building. "We're going there. And I don't know what's happening. Hopefully, we'll find out when we meet up with the rest of the team."

"Team?" she asked but was cut off when he practically yanked her arm out of its socket, dragging her toward the damaged apartment building.

Just as he started to climb a set of stairs leading up, five men came running down.

"Abandon ship," one of them said and raced past them.

"What's going on?" Graham asked.

"If the motorcade belongs to Koku, he's not here to schmooze with the locals," the second man down the stairs said. "He's here to destroy it and the people inside."

The man behind him continued speaking. "We think the trailer that just pulled up in front of the compound is full of explosives." He kept running.

A big blond guy with massive shoulders was the last one out. "Run!"

Graham and Angela raced after the departing men. As they neared the structure on the back side of the abandoned apartment building, an explosion rocked the ground, spewing chunks of concrete, rock and splinters of wood into the air.

Angela fell to the ground and covered the back of her neck.

Graham fell on top of her, using his body as a shield to protect her. When the debris stopped falling, he was back up, dragging her to her feet.

The rapid report of gunfire sounded behind them.

The men didn't stop until they reached a beat-up old van a couple blocks away.

The first guy there threw open the side door, leaped inside and crawled into the driver's seat. The others piled in after him.

When Angela reached the van, Graham lifted her and tossed her in like a load of laundry. He dived in behind her, landing on top of her, and someone slammed the door shut.

Angela could barely breathe with Graham's weight pressing her into the metal floor.

The popping noise of automatic weapons sounded close by.

"Go! Go! Go!" someone shouted.

The man behind the steering wheel shifted into Drive and spun out, leaving a layer of rubber on the street. Something hit the side of the vehicle.

Graham grunted and stiffened, letting out a string of curses.

Finally, he rolled off her and sat up.

Angela dragged in a deep breath, filling her lungs, and then pushed to a sitting position.

Two men sat in the seats up front. The bigger guy had sandy-blond hair. The driver had black hair. Three other men besides Graham crowded into the back, sitting or squatting with their backs to the walls of the van.

When her gaze came back around to Graham, he held his hand over his arm, his lips pressed tightly together.

"Damn, Buck, you're bleeding," one of the men said.

Angela looked again at the hand holding his arm. Blood leaked through his fingers and dripped onto the floor.

Her pulse leaped. "Why didn't you say something?"

"I was too busy getting off you so you could breathe," he said. "Besides, it's just a flesh wound."

Angela moved closer. "Let me see."

He removed his hand from the wound. Blood oozed from the injury, but not at an alarming rate. Still, she needed to stop the bleeding.

"Anyone have a knife?" she asked.

Four wicked-looking knives appeared in front of her.

She selected one, ripped the hem of the robe Buck wore and tore a length along the bottom all the way around. She folded it into a tight pad and applied it to the wound. "Use that to apply pressure."

Buck forced a smile. "Yes, ma'am."

She tore another length off the robe and used it to tie around his arm, knotting it over the wound to maintain the pressure. Some blood soaked through, but not enough for her to be worried about it.

"When we get back to the refugee camp, I'll sew you up."

"Let's get this straight," Graham said. "We're not going back to the refugee camp."

Angela stared around at the others. "But we have to. All of my equipment and supplies are there."

"We're not even supposed to be in South Sudan," said the big blond guy in the front seat. "We can't go to the refugee camp. We'd be too exposed and our mission would be jeopardized, if it hasn't already been." He glared at Graham.

Angela sensed he wasn't happy with her former boyfriend. But she couldn't be worried about that. She had a job to do. "Then let me out at the next corner," Angela said. "I'll get to the camp by myself."

Graham shook his head. "Not happening."

"What were you doing leading a protest against Koku?" the big guy in the front said. "Oh, and by the way, I'm Big Jake. Diesel's the one driving." He then pointed to a man with close-cropped brown hair leaning against the wall of the van. "That's Pitbull, and the one beside him is Harm." Harm had black hair and dark eyes. Big Jake nodded to the man in the very back with auburn hair and green eyes. "That's T-Mac. And I guess you met Buck."

"Buck?" She frowned at Graham.

Graham shrugged. "Short for Buckner."

"Do any of you have real names?" she asked.

"When we need them," Pitbull said.

T-Mac grinned. "On our paychecks."

"Well, Big Mac," Angela said. "I need to get back to the camp outside town, as soon as possible."

The men laughed.

"No can do," the man in the passenger seat said. "And it's Big Jake."

"Seriously, I have to go back. My nurse is there. If the raiders who attacked the government office make it out to the refugee camp, they might take her. So, if you're not taking me there, at least let me out and I'll walk." She moved toward the door and placed her fingers on the handle.

"Hey." Graham reached out with his injured arm and winced but grabbed her wrist anyway. "You can't jump out of a moving vehicle."

"If that's the only way to get back to the refugee camp, I'll do it. I won't leave my nurse to be terrorized, killed or sold into slavery." She spoke louder. "So if you don't stop this vehicle now, I'm going to jump."

Chapter Two

"Hold your horses. We'll take you to the camp," Diesel said. "Just let me get us far enough away from what's going on downtown."

"Jump from a moving vehicle?" Buck chuckled, then stopped when he realized Angela hadn't been kidding. He shook his head. "You're as stubborn as you always were."

Angela lifted her chin. "It's what keeps me going here. My stubbornness got me through medical school and my internship."

She didn't say it, but Buck could hear the comment she didn't make: *Unlike you.*

Buck felt the cut like a knife to his gut. "I had my reasons for leaving," he said and ended it there.

"Where's the refugee camp?" Diesel asked.

Angela turned away from Buck and focused her attention on Diesel. "Southwest of town."

Using less-traveled streets, Diesel drove the van

to the edge of town. Before they left the cover of the buildings for the open landscape, Big Jake glanced back.

"No one behind us for now," T-Mac confirmed.

Diesel shot out of Bentiu and into the open.

Not far from the town was the beginning of a city of tents and poorly erected shelters made of scrap plywood and tin.

"We can't drive right into camp," Big Jake said. "Remember, we're not supposed to be in this country."

Angela nodded. "Our tent is on the back side of the camp. There are some buildings past that where you can hide the van and let me off." She directed Diesel past the camp and a little farther, to where a stand of shanties stood.

Diesel parked behind one that appeared abandoned.

When Angela reached for the door, Buck gripped her wrist. "I'm going with you."

"There's no need," Angela said with her fingers curling around the handle. "I'm not coming back."

"The hell you aren't," Buck said.

"I'm not here to argue. I have to check on my nurse." She shoved the sliding door open and dropped to the ground. Without waiting, she took off toward the camp at a slow jog.

Buck shot a glance at Big Jake. "I can't let her go it alone."

Big Jake jerked his head toward Angela's departing figure. "Then go. We'll wait here as long as we're not discovered." He tapped the earbud headset. "Stay in touch. I'll send a couple men out to keep watch for bad guys."

"I'll keep you informed." Buck jumped out of the van and ran to catch up with Angela.

She didn't slow for him but kept jogging toward her destination. "You didn't have to follow me," she said. "I know what I'm doing."

"Humor me." He raised a hand to the makeshift bandage on his arm. "Besides, I need you to patch me up better."

"How do you know I didn't do a good job?"

"I'm the corpsman, the medic for the team. It's my professional opinion that you need to clean the wound and apply a fresh bandage to keep it from becoming infected."

Her eyes narrowed. "Right. You're a medic. Do it yourself."

"I can't perform surgery on myself, now can I?"

She sighed and kept moving. "Fine. It wouldn't hurt to clean the wound and apply sterile bandages."

Buck suppressed the smile threatening to spread across his face. He'd scored a very minor victory, but one that would give him a little more time to convince her to leave an extremely volatile area.

As they approached the sprawling camp, they circled around a large white tent to the entry at the front where a canvas sign was tied over the door. The red, white and black lettering stated Médecins Sans Frontières, which translated to Doctors Without Borders.

Buck knew all about this international nongovernmental organization known for humanitarian relief in war-torn or developing countries with little or no medical services available to the general population. He'd hoped one day to be one of the doctors to volunteer his time to help others less fortunate. He'd had lots of dreams when he'd started medical school.

A woman with graying blond hair stepped out of the tent and frowned when she saw Angela and Buck. "I heard an explosion in town. That wasn't anywhere close to your demonstration, was it?"

Angela's lips pressed together. "Brenda, we need to prep for stitches. I'll fill you in on what happened while we're sewing up this man."

Brenda smiled at Buck. "Hi, I'm Brenda Sites. And you are?"

"Graham Buckner, but you can call me Buck." He nodded toward the tent. "We don't have time for stitches," Buck said. "A clean pressure bandage will do for now."

Angela shook her head. "No, we need to close the wound to keep it from getting infected. I can do it in less than five minutes, if you'll shut up and let me get busy."

"All right, sweetheart. You don't have to be so bossy." Buck's lips twitched as he followed Angela into the tent, his gaze taking in the neat little hospital complete with a few beds and a separate room for more advanced procedures.

His curiosity always piqued when he was around medical equipment and medicine. More than anything, he wished he'd been able to finish his degree and residency. Alas, his past had caught up with him, and he'd had to leave school or risk exposing the people he cared most about to the murdering, scum-of-the-earth gang members he'd grown up with in Chicago.

He'd left school, Angela and his dreams behind to get away from his past and to get his past away from Angela. He couldn't regret that. She'd deserved to finish her schooling without being stalked, harassed and potentially harmed by Buck's old gang members.

The only way Buck had gotten the gang to leave him and Angela alone was to give up his dreams and leave Chicago all together.

"Have a seat." Angela indicated a folding chair in front of a small field desk.

"Really, we could just clean the wound, bandage it and be done in a lot less time," Buck said. "If you'll give me whatever you use to clean with, I can try to do it myself."

"Didn't you say you couldn't perform surgery on yourself?" Angela washed her hands, dried them and pulled on a pair of latex gloves, while her nurse spread out sterile drop cloths across the table, then laid out scissors, gauze, Betadine and tweezers. She used the scissors to remove the makeshift bandage from his arm. Blood oozed from the wound.

Angela inspected it. "See? You need stitches." She took over after the nurse completed removing the bandage and irrigated the wound with a syringe.

The nurse patted it dry with gauze and applied Betadine to the skin around the wound.

Angela threaded the needle with suture line, her movements quick and efficient. "We're short on local anesthetics. Hell, we're out of most medications." Angela met his gaze with a steady one of her own. "You'll have to hold very still and grin and bear it."

If he wasn't mistaken, she almost looked like she was enjoying taunting him with the threat of pain. He nodded. "Just do it quickly. We don't know when or if Koku's men will show up and cause more trouble."

Before the last word left his mouth, she stuck the needle into the edge of one side of the wound and looped it through the other. She talked softly as she worked, informing her nurse of what had occurred in Bentiu.

Buck stared at the top of Angela's head while bracing his jaw to keep from cursing. It hurt like hell, but he wouldn't jerk his hand away or let loose any of the choice words he wanted to say at that moment. Instead, he focused on Angela, taking advantage of her concentration on his arm to study her.

She hadn't changed much in their years apart. If anything, she'd become even more beautiful. Her dark hair framed her face, her olive-toned skin was a little darker and the confidence she exuded was palpable. The woman had matured into a self-assured, capable doctor with a steady hand.

Buck's heart swelled with pride for her. "I always knew you'd make it," he said softly.

Her hand stilled for a fraction of a second before she tied off the first stitch. "That's what happens when you stay focused."

Her comment hurt. He shouldn't have let it, but it did. Angela hadn't known how much he wanted to stay at school and be with her. He hadn't told her, figuring a clean break would be better than leaving her holding out hope for his return. "I had my reasons for leaving."

"Yeah. And it doesn't matter, does it? You left. I

stayed. We lived our own lives." She slipped the needle into another section of the wound. "Separately."

Buck winced and bit down on his tongue. He figured Angela was right. Why bother rehashing the past? It was over. What he needed to do was concentrate on getting her out of the camp before Koku's men came looking for another place to shake up.

Angela and Brenda worked on his arm with quiet efficiency.

By the time Angela tied off the last stitch, Buck could swear he'd ground at least a quarter of an inch off his back teeth. He released the breath he'd held and stood.

"Now, let's get you out of here." Buck reached for her wrist.

Angela stepped backward, avoiding his hand. "I told you, I'm not going. I can't leave these people."

"You saw what happened in Bentiu. Those guys could come here next."

"These people need us. We can't abandon them." Angela peeled the gloves from her hands.

Buck's jaw tightened. He couldn't walk away and leave her here, in danger. "You're not safe."

"*They're* not safe." She laid the gloves on the table and captured his gaze in an unflinching one of her own. "I'm not going."

Big Jake's voice came over Buck's headset. "We've got company."

"You may not have a choice," Buck said. "My guys say Koku's men are coming into camp as we speak."

No sooner had he made the announcement than a burst of gunfire could be heard outside, followed by women screaming.

"If you don't leave for *me*—" Buck nodded toward her nurse "—leave for Brenda. We need to get both of you out of here. Now." He took Angela's hand and dragged her toward the door.

More gunfire erupted.

Angela dug in her heels and pulled her hand free. "You're a SEAL. You can stop them."

"Not if we're outnumbered. And sometimes that only causes more casualties when so many civilians are involved."

"Seriously, guys," Big Jake said into Buck's ear. "They're headed straight for your tent."

"My men say Koku's men are headed directly for this tent. Are you coming with me or staying to argue with a killer?"

ANGELA HAD SPENT so much of her time working with and healing the people in the refugee camp. To leave them would be like abandoning her own children.

"Dr. Vega." Brenda touched her arm, her eyes rounded, her hand shaking. "We can't help anyone if we're dead."

Her nurse's words hit hard. If Brenda was scared, Angela owed it to her to get her out. She turned to Buck. "Take my nurse and get her to safety."

He shook his head. "I'm not leaving without you."

One of the women Angela had been training to assist with medical treatments ran into the tent. "Dr. Angela! Dr. Angela! The men. They're coming for you. They're coming for the doctor." She took Angela's arm and hauled her toward the door. "You have to go. You go. Now."

Angela's gaze met Buck's over the woman's head. "Okay. We'll go."

Buck touched his headset. "We're on our way." He stepped in front of Angela before she could leave the tent. "But not that way." He pulled his Ka-Bar knife from the sheath on his belt and strode through the tent to the back, where he jabbed the knife into the fabric and slit an opening large enough for a person to get through.

Then he stepped out and held the fabric wide. "Now you," he said, waving for Brenda to come next.

The nurse ducked through and moved out of the way.

While Buck and Brenda were making their way

out of the tent, Angela got busy throwing equipment, supplies and medication into her backpack.

Buck stuck his head back into the tent. "Angela, we have to go now. They're almost on us."

Angela shot one final glance around the tent she'd called home for the past six months, tossed in a couple bottles of water and dived out of the tent.

Loud voices could be heard from the men storming through the refugee camp toward the hospital tent.

Her heart thundering against her ribs, Angela ran.

Buck grabbed the backpack from her arm and slung it over his shoulder. Then he took her hand and urged her to go faster.

By the time they reached the deserted shack, Angela could barely breathe. T-Mac and Harm were waiting at the sliding door, where they lifted Brenda off her feet and into the van. They did the same for Angela and then clambered in after them. Buck was last inside, slamming the door as the vehicle took off.

Angela stared through the back window of the van at the camp she was leaving behind. Smoke rose from the tent they'd just vacated, the fabric succumbing to the flames shooting into the sky.

Men in black clothing ran toward them, firing their rifles.

But by then, the van was far enough away, and the bullets fell short.

"We don't have much of a lead on them," Buck said. "Once they get their trucks rolling, they'll be after us."

"Then we need to keep rolling," Big Jake said. "The faster, the better."

Diesel pressed his foot to the accelerator, taking the van as fast as it would go, fully loaded with SEALs and the women.

"If we're lucky, the sun will set before they catch up to us," Big Jake said. "The 160th is on standby for extraction as soon as we give them the coordinates."

"In the meantime," Diesel tossed over his shoulder, "any suggestions on a place around here to hide a van and eight people?"

Angela thought hard. For the most part, she'd been confined to the hospital tent, working nonstop with masses of people living in the terrible conditions of the refugee camp. But there was one time she and Brenda had been asked to help a village elder in another small town nearby. She glanced out the window. They were headed that direction. "I know of a place."

Leaning through the gap between the two front seats, she watched the road ahead, trying to remember where they'd turned to get to the village.

Brenda squeezed in next to her. "Are you taking them to Abu Hanafi's village?"

She nodded. "The turnoff to the village should be coming up soon."

"Remember, it was where the abandoned tank tracks were," Brenda said.

"Right." Angela turned to Diesel. "There should be some buildings coming up soon and a field beside the road with what looks like a pile of junk metal. It's actually the tracks from an army tank."

Diesel nodded. "I'll be on the lookout."

Angela glanced back through the van's rear window, her pulse pounding. As she turned back to the front, her gaze skimmed across Buck. Her heart did a backflip. When she'd first realized who'd plucked her out of the middle of the protest, she'd been too angry to fully appreciate what had happened.

In this totally different part of the world, why had fate brought Graham back to her? At that very moment?

He was the same Graham she'd known and loved in medical school, yet different.

His body was honed, his muscles tight and strong, and his eyes…those gorgeous blue eyes she'd fallen into on their first group project were somehow different. Although still the same blue, they appeared to see more and have more depth than before. The lines around the corners of his eyes added character, and the scar on his chin made her want to reach out and touch it.

As quickly as the thought sprang into her mind, she pushed it away and returned her attention to the road in front of the van.

Ahead, on the left, was a field of long grass with a patch of dirt next to the road. Rusted metal lay in a heap in the middle of the dirt.

"There!" Angela pointed to the dirt road past the tank track. "Turn there."

Diesel only slowed enough to negotiate the turn and then sped along the bumpy road, barely more than a rutted track.

Big Jake's brow crinkled as he glanced her way. "Are you sure this is the way?"

"Positive." She nodded toward a blue tin shack. "I remember that blue building."

"And the one with the orange roof," Brenda added, pointing to the structure.

"The village is another mile or more along this road, and it's tucked into the side of a hill."

"As long as the dust settles before the rebel attackers get to where we turned off, they won't have a clue we came this way."

"*If* the dust settles," T-Mac said.

Angela glanced back at the cloud of dust rising up behind them.

Buck touched her arm. "It'll settle."

She gave him a hint of a smile and turned away. So many forgotten emotions welled up inside her. Why did he have to come back into her life? Why now? But if he hadn't, she might be dead. The protest she'd staged against the local government could have ended a lot worse. She prayed the women who'd gone along with her had made it back to safety.

Leaving behind the refugees she'd grown to care for was killing her. But like Brenda had said, she couldn't help people if she was dead.

Soon, they came to the little village tucked into the side of a hill. Shacks and huts lined the road, with barely clothed children playing outside.

"Let me out," Angela said. "I'll speak to Abu Hanafi. He might not want us in his village if we bring trouble with us."

"Tell him we won't stay any longer than it takes to get airlifted out," Big Jake said. "And we'll arrange pickup away from his village so as not to draw too much attention to it."

Angela nodded and hopped out of the van. Buck followed.

"It might be better if I go alone," Angela said.

"Not happening." He gripped her elbow and marched forward.

Angela shrugged free of his hand. Every time he touched her, that same jolt, like an electrical current, ran through her, reminding her of the connection they'd had when they were much younger.

She tightened her jaw. That was the past. "I got along fine without you for six months in this country. I can do this on my own."

"Then do it on your own, just with me. I won't say a word. You'll barely know I'm there."

She snorted. "You're over six feet tall. Much taller than many of the people in this village. I think I'll notice you. And I won't be the only one." As much as she protested, she did feel protected when he was around.

Angela led the way to the mud-and-stick building at the center of the little village. A woman wearing a faded red-and-gold dress with a red scarf draped over her head and shoulders stood in the doorway with a toddler on her hip.

With a smile, Angela addressed the daughter of the village elder. "Uluru, how are you and your children?"

She knew from the last time she'd been here that Uluru spoke perfect English she'd learned at a missionary school when she was much younger. At twenty-one years old, she had three children, the youngest of which she was holding.

"They are well. I am teaching Kamal his letters. He will go to school one day."

Angela nodded. "Your children will be smart as well as beautiful, like their mother."

She snorted softly. "If they live that long and are not stolen away by Koku's army." Uluru moved out of the doorway. "You are here to see my father?"

"Yes," Angela said.

"And this man with you, who dresses like one of our men?"

"He is my…" Angela almost said *boyfriend*, but that was so many years ago.

"I'm her fiancé," Buck said and cupped Angela's elbow. "We are to be married soon."

Angela swallowed hard to keep from disagreeing out loud. Now that he'd said it, she couldn't deny it without appearing wishy-washy in front of Uluru and her father.

Uluru's gaze swept over Buck from head to toe before she nodded. "As the doctor's betrothed, you are welcome in our home."

Inside, the structure was cast in shadow, with no electrical lighting in use.

Uluru passed through the house and out into a small courtyard where an old man, dressed all in white much like Buck, sat cross-legged on the ground in the shade of a tree.

Angela waited for the man to invite her forward.

When he did, she sat cross-legged across from him, and Buck sat beside her.

Uluru joined them, setting the toddler on his feet. The child wandered off to play with a stick.

Angela studied the man, searching his face for any signs of illness. "You are well?" she asked.

Abu Hanafi nodded, his gaze going to Buck and back to Angela. "Who is this white man who dresses like one of our people?"

Buck sat up straight, meeting the man's gaze with a strength and confidence Angela had to admire. "I am Dr. Vega's fiancé."

The elder continued to stare at Buck for a long moment, as if sizing him up. Finally, he gave a single nod. "Why are you here?"

Angela realized the elder wasn't speaking to her, but to Buck. In deference, she let Buck respond.

"There was an attack on the government building in Bentiu. We believe it was Koku. Then his men attacked the refugee camp," Buck said. "My men and I got Dr. Vega and her nurse out before they could be harmed. We all need a place to hide until after the sun sets, at which time we will leave."

Abu Hanafi's brow furrowed. "You have brought danger to my village?"

"We hope not," Buck said. "But we will leave as soon as we can."

"Or we could leave now, if you think we have endangered your people," Angela said softly.

A long silence stretched between the elder, Angela and Buck. Finally, Abu Hanafi nodded. "You will stay until dark. However, if trouble follows you, you will leave sooner. Too many of our children have been stolen by Koku and his men."

"Koku has taken children from your village?" Buck questioned.

"He takes our young boys to fill his army," the elder said. "We are forced to hide them in the bushes when Koku is in the area."

"I'm sorry to hear that," Angela said. "I wish we could do something to stop him."

"You have to know where to find him," Buck said, "in order to do anything to stop him."

Once again, Abu Hanafi studied Buck. "You are not a doctor."

Buck shook his head. "No, sir."

"You are an American soldier?"

Buck tensed beside Angela. "No, sir."

That penetrating gaze pinned Buck to his spot. But Buck wasn't giving the man any more than he already had. "Sir, we should move our vehicle before Koku's people see it and report back to him."

Abu Hanafi waved his hand. "Go."

When Angela rose to her feet, he touched her arm. "My people owe you a debt we cannot repay."

"You owe me nothing," Angela assured him.

The elder dipped his head. "I can only repay you in friendship."

"Which is the most important payment of all." She held out her hand to the man. He took it in both of his. "Thank you for saving my life."

"You're welcome."

Uluru led them through the house and back to the van. "You can park in the trees at the base of the bluff," she said.

"Thank you." Angela strode back to the van, anxious to get away from Buck and the chemistry he seemed to be stirring up inside her. The faster they resolved the issue with Koku, the quicker she could get back to helping others.

She hoped it happened sooner rather than later, because all those old feelings she'd had back in medical school seemed to be bubbling up inside. Losing him the first time had been bad enough. She feared the more time she spent with Buck, the more dangerous he became.

To her heart.

Chapter Three

Buck and Angela returned to the van, where several of the SEALs stood outside the vehicle.

Having taken over the conversation with Abu Hanafi, Buck allowed Angela to take the lead this time.

"We can stay only until after dark," Angela jumped in without preamble. After informing them of where Uluru had indicated they could park the van out of sight of the road, Angela announced, "I'll walk."

"I'll walk with you," Buck said.

The only hint she wasn't happy with his announcement was the tightening of her lips. "Suit yourself." And she started toward the hillside.

Diesel cranked the van's engine, the SEALs piled in and the van passed Angela and Buck on the way to the hiding place.

Angela waited until the people in the van were

well out of hearing distance before she said, "Did you ever consider I might not want you to walk with me?"

"Yes." He lifted a shoulder. "And I ignored it. I don't feel comfortable leaving you anywhere alone."

"You left me in Chicago," she shot back.

The anger and hurt in Angela's voice twisted a knife in Buck's gut. "We're in South Sudan, a volatile nation filled with murderous people" was all he could push past the tightness in his throat.

"Like Chicago?" Again, she was quick with her comebacks. Sadly, she was right.

"I had reasons for leaving when I did," he said.

Angela spun around in front of him, stopping him in his tracks. "I wouldn't know, now would I?" She poked a finger at his chest. "Because you didn't bother to tell me what they were, or even that you were leaving. I had to find out from your roommate, *after* you were long gone." She smacked her palm flat against his chest. "You'd think any kind of man would have the decency to tell his girlfriend he was skipping town, quitting college and joining the navy. But then, you weren't even decent—"

Buck grabbed the woman's arms and yanked her against him, crushing her lips with a bruising kiss. He'd never wanted to leave her, would rather have slit his own throat than hurt her. And now, seeing her in front of him, her eyes alight with fury, her cheeks blooming with righteous indignation, he couldn't resist.

This was the woman he'd never been able to forget. The kiss started out raw and angry but quickly turned hungry and desperate. He remembered her lips, the way they felt beneath his mouth, the curve of her body against his and the way she leaned into him when she gave her whole self to the kiss.

At first she was stiff in his arms, her palms on his chest. But she didn't push him away. Slowly, almost imperceptibly, she loosened up until she was leaning into him, giving back every bit as much as he gave.

When at last he was forced to surface for air, he drew in a deep breath and rested his forehead against hers.

"Don't think this changes anything," she said, her fingers curling into his shirt. "I'm still angry with you. And I'm still staying in Sudan." Then she did push out of his arms, turned and ran after the van.

Buck followed at a slower pace, wondering what the hell had just happened. He'd never intended to pick up where they'd left off all those years ago. Angela had her life, and he had his. Nothing between them would ever work.

Granted, Chicago was not an issue anymore. From what he understood, his old gang had been disbanded with the arrest and incarceration of their leader. The man had finally been caught and convicted of murder.

Once the team had the van hidden behind old buildings and trees near the base of the hillside, they climbed out and prepared to lie low until after sunset.

Harm and Diesel went south, and Pitbull hiked to the north, each going around the hill. Big Jake and T-Mac climbed to the top, all of them searching for potential threats and the coordinates to give the helicopter crew for their extraction.

They left Buck to guard the two women.

"Tough job, but someone has to do it," Diesel said as he left with Harm.

Word must have gotten out that the doctor was in the village. Before long, women brought children to the base of the hillside, seeking assistance for minor injuries, skin infections, lacerations and more.

Working out of the side door of the van, Angela, Brenda and Buck treated the patients.

All the while, Buck kept a close watch on the surrounding area and scrutinized every patient, searching for hidden weapons. But they were all what they appeared to be...people sincerely in need of help.

As the sun dropped to the horizon, the line of people dwindled to two, then one.

The last one, a bone-thin woman dressed in a faded gold dress and scarf, waited to speak until the others had all gone. "Dr. Angela, you must come with me." She took Angela's hand and tried to drag her away.

Buck stepped between them and loosened the woman's grip on Angela's hand. "The doctor isn't going anywhere. What do you want?"

"She must come," the woman insisted.

Angela placed a hand on Buck's arm and stepped around him. "What's your name?"

"I am Fatima." She turned, waving her hand to the side. "Please, you must come."

"Can't we talk about your problem here?" Angela asked.

"Not me," Fatima said. "My son needs you."

Angela frowned. "What's wrong with your son?"

Fatima glanced around furtively. "He is injured."

"How was he injured?" Angela asked.

The woman looked from Angela to Buck and over her shoulder, as if afraid of something or someone. "Please, my son needs your help."

The sun had set, and the grayness of dusk enveloped them.

Big Jake, T-Mac, Harm, Diesel and Pitbull all appeared out of the shadows.

"What's going on?" Diesel asked.

Buck tilted his head toward Fatima. "This woman wants the doctor to go to her son."

"I don't recommend it." Big Jake glanced down at his watch. "Our extraction is scheduled for T-minus five minutes. We'd better move to the other side of the hill. And make it fast."

The men headed in that direction. Buck started to follow, but Angela wasn't at his side.

She stood with her feet planted firmly on the ground. "I can't leave this woman without help."

"You can't stay," Buck said. "Koku could be back at any moment."

"Please…" The woman took Angela's hand again, her eyes pleading. "My son is injured. He needs your help. He has been beaten by Koku's men."

Even Buck, a hardened SEAL, couldn't ignore the woman's desperation. "How far is it to your son?"

"On the other side of the village. It will not take long. He has suffered so much. Please help him."

The thumping sound of rotors beating the air made Buck's heart leap. Their transport neared. "We can't do this," he said to Angela.

She stared up into his eyes. "I can't *not* do this."

Buck turned to the woman. "Can you bring your son here?"

"No. My son traveled a long way. He escaped from Koku's camp. His action is punishable by death. He cannot risk being seen and recaptured."

"Wait." Buck's heart rate ratcheted up. "Your son escaped from Koku's camp?"

She nodded. "It is very bad there. He does not wish to return."

Excitement rose like a tidal wave in Buck. "But he knows where Koku lives?"

The woman frowned. "Yes, but he does not wish to return," she repeated. "He was one of many young boys taken to fill Koku's army."

Angela squeezed the woman's hand. "I will help."

Big Jake trotted back to where Buck and Angela stood. "Hey, are you two coming? We have to get around this hill to our extraction point. It's time to move out."

Buck turned to Big Jake. "This woman's son escaped Koku's camp. He knows where we can find Koku."

Big Jake frowned, and he stared at the woman in the deepening dusk. "Your son knows where Koku lives?"

The woman nodded.

Big Jake glanced at his watch. "We'll have to come back to follow up. Right now, we're scheduled for extraction."

"And you need to go and take my nurse back to safety," Angela said. "But I'm staying to help this woman's son."

Big Jake's frown deepened. "I can't force you to come with us. But you realize the risk you're taking?"

She nodded. "I do."

"And I'm staying with her," Buck said.

"You can't," Big Jake said. "You're part of the team. We leave no man behind."

"Give me the radio. I'll be a one-man recon element scouting out Koku's location." Buck talked fast, the idea coming to him as he spoke. "When you get the nurse to a safe location, you can come back. Hopefully by then, I'll have Koku's exact coordinates. We can complete our mission."

For a long moment, Big Jake stared at Buck. Finally, he said, "I don't like it."

"You don't have to like it, but it makes sense for me to go with this woman and check out her son's story. If it pans out, we'll get a lot farther a lot faster than we have in the past week." Buck nodded toward the sound of the approaching helicopter. "You need to hurry. They won't wait long."

Big Jake nodded to T-Mac. "Give him your ground-to-air radio and go."

T-Mac unclipped the radio from his belt and handed it over to Buck. "Don't do anything to get yourself killed." T-Mac spun and ran toward the sound of the helicopter.

Big Jake stuck out his hand. "What T-Mac said."

Buck clasped the man's hand and was pulled into a bear hug.

Then Big Jake was gone, running after T-Mac.

Buck watched as the last two men of his team disappeared around the side of the hill. Moments later, the thumping sound of the rotor blades intensified and then faded into the distance.

For all intents and purposes, Buck was stranded in South Sudan, without his team to provide backup. Whatever happened from here on, he'd be on his own until he called for extraction. His lifeline was the radio in his hand.

"Please," the woman said. "My son needs you."

Angela slipped her backpack of supplies over one shoulder and said in a calm, quiet voice, "Show me the way."

Buck grabbed his gear bag from the back of the van. Keeping a close watch on his surroundings, he followed.

ANGELA COULDN'T BELIEVE Buck had actually remained behind with her. She hadn't expected him to. Hell, she hadn't really thought through her *own* plan. All she knew was that she couldn't let some poor injured boy lie in pain because she was in a hurry to get out of the country.

Fatima skirted the village, keeping to the deepest shadows that a night sky full of stars couldn't penetrate. Once they were past the jumble of huts and tin shacks, she led them another half mile to what appeared to be a huge junk pile of tin and scraps of worm-eaten lumber.

When she pushed aside a sheet of corrugated roofing metal, she waved for Angela to enter.

The small cave-like structure's interior was pitch-black. Angela hesitated at the entrance, trying to remember whether or not she'd brought a flashlight in the backpack she'd hastily loaded.

A soft click sounded and a beam of light cut through the darkness.

She smiled. Trust Buck to have a flashlight handy. He'd always been good about being prepared. He must have been a Boy Scout in a past life.

He stepped around her and shined the light into the structure.

A young boy, around ten years old, lay on a pile of rags, his face caked with dried blood, one of his arms bent at an odd angle.

The shack was small and rickety. Angela didn't know how she'd manage to work on the boy in the cramped space. When she bent to enter, a hand shot out to stop her.

"We'll have to move him out into the open," Buck

said. "This hut doesn't look like it'll stand up to a strong wind."

"I'm smaller. Let me move him," Angela said.

"No way." Buck handed her the flashlight. "Just give me some light to work in."

Angela held the beam steady as Buck hunched over and ducked into the shack.

The boy moaned but didn't fight when Buck gently laid his injured arm over his chest. Then he lifted him into his arms and maneuvered the child and his own big body through the narrow entrance and out into the balmy night air.

Fatima spread her scarf on the ground. "Place him here."

Buck eased the boy to the ground, careful not to jolt his arm or cause him more pain.

His mother hovered close by, looking over her shoulder, fear evident in the whites of her eyes. "You will fix this?" She pointed to the boy's bent arm.

"I'll have to reset the bone. It's going to hurt. What is your name?" Angela asked the boy.

When the boy didn't answer right away, Fatima twisted her hands together. "He is Mustafa."

Using the flashlight, Angela shined the beam into the boy's eyes, testing his pupils' response. No indications of concussion, despite the blood on his head and face. She checked his vital signs. His pulse was strong, his blood pressure right for his size and age. "Mustafa," she said, her tone low, calm and gentle. "What I'm about to do will hurt, but then your arm will feel better. Do you understand?"

The boy nodded, probably in too much pain to do more.

Over the light's beam, Angela caught Buck's attention. "You'll have to hold his upper arm while I apply traction."

He nodded, sat behind the boy and leaned over to grip the child's skinny arm. "Ready."

Angela slowly straightened the arm.

The boy bared his teeth in silence, his body tensing.

Once she had it straight, Angela pulled gently but firmly until the bone jutting at an odd angle beneath the skin moved back in line with the other end.

Mustafa's back arched and his jaw clenched to keep him from crying out.

Angela hated to cause another human so much pain, but she knew it was necessary and that he'd feel better once they were done.

The boy squirmed and squeezed his eyes closed, perspiration shining on his forehead. Then he went limp.

"I believe he passed out," Buck whispered.

"Good, then maybe he won't be in as much pain."

She continued to apply strong downward pressure, easing the bone back into place. Once she had the bone where she wanted it, she held the arm steady. "I need something for a splint."

"Do you have him?" Buck asked.

"Yes," she said. "Go."

Buck released the boy's shoulder and took the flashlight. A few moments later, he came back with two flat, straight sticks about the length of the boy's forearm. He laid them on the ground beside Angela and dug in her backpack for roller gauze and scissors.

While Angela held the arm and spoke to the boy in a soft monotone voice, Buck placed the two flat sticks on either side of the boy's arm and wrapped the roller gauze around and around until he was certain it would be sufficient to keep the arm immobile. When he finished, he cut the gauze and secured the end.

"Well done," Angela said. "You look like you've done this before."

He shrugged. "Like I said, I'm the team medic. We've had a few bumps, bruises and broken bones."

Angela nodded. She would bet he'd seen a lot more than that, including gunshot and shrapnel wounds.

The boy woke before they finished and watched the proceedings with interest, no longer tense with pain.

Angela gave him a mild painkiller and one of the

bottles of water she'd stashed in her bag. "He should sleep now."

Buck touched her arm and motioned for her to move away from the boy and his mother. "We need to question him about Koku's location before he goes to sleep."

He leaned so close to her, she could feel the warmth of his body. A shiver of awareness slipped across her skin. She almost didn't register what he said. "He's been through a lot."

"We can't wait. We don't know if Koku will come back through tonight or tomorrow looking for the van and the people who were in it."

Still, Angela hated to disturb the boy. He'd been in so much pain.

"I know you want your patient to recover, but we also put the people of this village at risk just by being here," Buck reasoned. "We need to leave as soon as possible. Preferably at night, to avoid being seen in that van."

Angela knew he was right. The longer she held off questioning the child, the more likely he'd fall asleep before they could. "Fine. Question him. But how is a child going to be able to give you directions?"

"I don't know, but I have to try." He returned to the boy and squatted on the ground beside him. "Are you thirsty?"

Mustafa nodded.

In the glow of the flashlight, Buck held the bottle of water to the boy's mouth. When he'd had enough, Buck capped it and set it beside the child. "Mustafa, your mother says you were in Koku's camp?"

The boy's eyes widened and his gaze darted around.

"It's okay." Buck rested a hand on the boy's arm. "We won't take you back there. But we want to know where to find Koku. Can you tell us how to get there?"

The boy's eyes closed for a moment.

Angela thought he'd gone to sleep. Then he opened them and nodded. "I will show you." He sat up with help from Buck, leaned over the side of the scarf he lay on and drew his finger in the dirt.

"It is a long way. Ten days' walking." He dragged his finger in a fairly straight line for a while, then he poked a dot next to the line. "There are one...two—" he poked another dot, then another "—three...four... five villages along the way. The first one is very small, even smaller than my village. The second one is small, too. The third is a town with a church at the center. The missionaries have gone, and the building has been damaged, but it still stands, and it gave me shelter for one night."

Again, the boy's eyes closed and he grew silent.

Then he opened his eyes as if doing so took great effort. "The next two villages are very much the same as the first—small. The fourth one has an old abandoned truck beside the road—black, like fire burned it. I slept beneath it one day to hide from sight of Koku's soldiers."

Angela's heart squeezed in her chest at the thought of the little boy hiding beneath the burned-out hull of a truck, fearing for his life. He shouldn't have to be afraid. He should be in school learning to read and write. He should be playing with his friends, able to be a kid for a while longer. Her eyes burned with the hint of tears.

"The fifth town is much larger, like Bentiu, with buildings, houses, stores. There are many of Koku's men in those streets. It was not safe. I did not enter. I hid in the bushes outside the town. When the sky became dark, I circled the town and continued to follow the road all the way back to my home."

"After the big town, is that where we will find Koku's camp?"

The boy shook his head. "There is a place where the one road becomes two." Mustafa drew a fork in the road that formed a Y. "To get to Koku's camp, you must take this road." He pointed at the fork to the left. "I watched when we were taken. I knew that if I escaped, I would have to know the way to return to my home." The boy lifted his chin. "Koku's camp is another day's walking from the fork in the road. Half of a day on the road, another half heading west into the setting sun on a smaller, rougher road, leading into the hills."

His mother laid a hand on his shoulder. "My son is all I have. If we have to, we will leave our home and find another place to live."

"You might need to," Buck advised. "If Koku learns we were here, he might search the entire village and surrounding area."

After treating so many patients and then having a helicopter land on the back side of the hill where the village was situated, it would be hard to keep the secret that an American doctor and six military men had been there.

For the villagers' sake, Angela hoped Koku didn't find out. But she wasn't banking on it. Now that she had Mustafa on the road to recovery, she realized it was time to move on. And like Buck had said, moving at night made the most sense.

Buck. Calling him Buck made it seem like he was a different person from the one she'd known back in medical school. Perhaps it would help to keep her from falling for him all over again.

Angela gave Mustafa and his mother instructions

on how to take care of the broken arm until it was fully healed in six to eight weeks.

Then Buck helped Mustafa into the ramshackle hut, tried to shore up the posts holding the roof up and stepped out.

Angela turned to the boy's mother. "Fatima, will you be all right taking care of Mustafa?"

The woman nodded. "Now that Mustafa is home, we will make sure we he is not captured again."

Angela glanced at the hut where the boy lay nestled in the darkness. She understood what would happen to the boy should he be recaptured. Most likely, he'd be shot or tortured to death as a message to others who might attempt escape.

Buck cupped her elbow, his touch sending a spark through her system. "We need to go before the light of dawn," he said.

Having done all she could for the child, Angela nodded and followed Buck back toward the village.

When they reached the van, a ghostly figure in white robes hovered by the driver's side. As they neared, the starlight revealed their visitor as Abu Hanafi.

His face was grave. "You said you would be gone by now."

Angela stepped forward. "We are the last two to leave. We will be gone soon."

When Buck tried to get around the elder to the driver's door, the man stood in his way. "This van will be recognized if you try to take it now," Abu Hanafi said.

"It's the only transportation we have," Buck said.

"You have helped my people. I would help you with an alternative to the van."

Angela shot a glance toward Buck. "What alternative?"

"Follow me." Abu Hanafi led the way to a mud-and-stick hut on the edge of the village. Unlike most huts, this one had a sturdy door with a lock hanging from a hasp. The elder used a key to unlock the mechanism.

Buck switched on his flashlight.

The hut contained a variety of items, including sacks of grain, seed and farm implements. In the far corner of the hut stood a relatively large item covered in old cloth.

The village elder grabbed the end of the cloth and yanked it to the side, revealing a shiny red racing motorcycle beneath.

"Uh…this?" Angela shook her head. "I don't think so."

"The van belongs to you?" Abu Hanafi asked Buck.

Buck nodded. "We paid cash for it."

"The motorcycle was a gift from a man we helped hide over a year ago. We haven't used it. I cannot drive it. What we need more is a van for the people of this village. I would trade the motorcycle for the van." The elder's eyes narrowed as he stared across at Buck. "You know how to ride a motorcycle?"

"Yes, sir." Buck grinned. "Although it wasn't as nice as this one, I had one when I was in college."

A smile tugged at Angela's lips at the memory. "I know. You took me on several dates on the back of that bike." Angela crossed her arms over her chest. "But we're talking South Sudan, not Chicago." She waved toward the bike. "There's no protection against bullets."

"Bullets can go through the metal of the van," Buck countered. "Besides, this will be faster. And if we're being chased by men in trucks, we could go off-road and get away much more easily than in the van."

Everything he said was correct. The motorcycle would make it easier and faster to get around. A big van would be far too noticeable and hard to hide. As much as she hated the thought of traveling in this fashion, she could see its merit.

"What do you say?" Buck asked.

She drew in a deep breath and let it out slowly. "Thank you, Abu Hanafi. We accept your offer."

Chapter Four

Buck walked the bike out into the open and then checked out the motor, the wires and the brakes. He filled the tank from the fuel jugs the elder had on hand and cranked the engine. It started on the second try and roared to life.

He breathed a sigh of relief. If a motorcycle sat unused for too long, the carburetor often gummed up. But the engine ran smoothly. It would use less fuel and get them around in places a van might not be able to go.

All that was left to do was strap his gear bag and Angela's backpack to the back of the bike and climb on.

After securing their bags, Buck got on first, straddling the seat with both feet on the ground to balance. The engine was powerful enough to handle two riders and not lose speed or degrade the bike's ability to make turns.

Angela's gaze went from the bike to the man and the gear. "Are you sure there's room for me?"

Buck scooted forward. "It'll be tight, but doable." He tipped his head to the side. "Hop on."

With a deep breath, she slid her leg over the seat and placed her feet on the footrests. She couldn't get any closer to Buck unless they were both naked. His pulse sped and his body heated everywhere it touched hers. Which was just about everywhere from his thighs to his back.

"This isn't going to work." Angela started to get off.

He put out his hand, stopping her. "It'll work. I promise."

She sat down hard, but at least she didn't get off. "You could just leave me here and come back for me when you're done scouting," she suggested.

"I don't dare leave you. After they torched your tent at the refugee camp, I don't trust what Koku would do to you if he found you here, unprotected."

Angela shivered. "You have a point. I don't have to like it, but it makes sense."

Buck handed over the keys to the van to Abu Hanafi. "I don't suppose you have helmets?" he asked the elder.

Angela latched on to the only excuse that seemed

within her reach. "Ah, see? We shouldn't take the bike. It's too dangerous to ride without a helmet."

Abu Hanafi darted to the corner and unearthed one red helmet that matched the bike. "I have only one."

"Hopefully, it'll fit Dr. Vega." Buck twisted around to help the elder fit the helmet over Angela's head and buckle the strap beneath her chin.

It fit perfectly, and she was so darned cute with the frown on her face framed by the helmet. Before he could resist, he bent forward and kissed the tip of her nose. "You'll be all right." Then he pulled the face shield down over the front and straightened to address the elder. "Thank you for your assistance. We hope we don't cause your people trouble by having been here." He reached out a hand.

Abu Hanafi shook it and let go. "You need to go before the sun rises."

Buck checked his watch. They had a couple hours before dawn, but they needed to get as far down the road as possible before stopping for the day. They'd have to do all of their movement at night to stay under Koku's radar.

"Ready?" he said.

"No." Angela sighed. "Yes."

Although Buck eased the throttle on the handle, the powerful motorcycle still leaped forward. Angela squealed and flung her arms around his waist to hold on.

Buck chuckled as he pulled away from the village and onto the road leading south, the direction from which Mustafa had said he'd come.

Angela might be better off hiding in the village, but Buck couldn't leave her. Though Abu Hanafi had offered them shelter and a place to hide, he could do nothing against Koku's armed men. And Buck didn't want to imagine what would happen to Angela should Koku find her in the village. Would they respect the fact that she was a doctor? Or just look at her as a woman to be handled any way they wanted?

Buck wasn't willing to test any theory involving Koku, his men and Angela. He'd take care of Angela and do his best to keep her safe.

He drove the motorcycle along the main road without using the headlights. The stars shining down from the heavens provided sufficient illumination to see the road and any obstacles in the way. No one stirred in the huts they passed on their way out of the village, and soon, they left the village behind.

The nights were cooler than the heat of the day. Buck preferred to travel through the countryside at night when most people slept. However, he had to be wary of animals wandering across the road. No sooner had he picked up a decent amount of speed than he had to slam on the brakes to avoid plowing into one of the long-horned cows the Dinka people raised. It lay in the middle of the dusty road along with twenty more.

Buck wove through the herd, careful not to get too close to the horns or to run over or disturb them enough to start a stampede.

Angela clung to him, her hands locked around his waist as he leaned left, then right, then left again. She was getting better at going with the motion of his body and maintaining the correct balance to keep the bike from falling over.

Once past the herd, Buck picked up speed. Already the sky was lightening in the east, the gray glow of predawn creeping over the horizon. They would have to stop soon or risk being seen.

Buck slowed, taking time to scout out a good rest stop. On the outskirts of the second small town Mustafa had described, Buck found a small knoll several yards off the main road. It was surrounded by bushes, leafy trees and nothing else that he could see in the early-morning light.

He drove off the road and across a grassy field to reach the knoll.

Angela must have fallen asleep, because she jerked upright and said, "What? What's happening?"

He briefly covered her hand with his. "We're stopping before sunrise."

"Can't we keep going?"

"Not if we want to remain undetected. Besides, we both need some sleep."

She yawned and nodded, her helmet bumping against his back. "I suppose so. You must be exhausted."

As they reached the knoll, Buck brought the motorcycle to a stop. "Think you can stand while I stash the bike in the bushes?"

"Of course I can stand," she said confidently.

"Go easy. You're not used to riding for a long time. It can be hard on a body."

She slipped to the side and planted her foot on the ground, then brought the other leg over the top. Immediately her knees buckled.

Buck reached out to catch her before she fell and pulled her against him with one arm, while the other balanced the motorcycle. He chuckled softly. He couldn't get over how good she felt pressed against his chest.

He loosened the strap beneath her chin and slid the helmet off her head. "A little wobbly?"

She laughed. "A little. Ouch. I didn't realize how sore I'd gotten until I moved."

"I'll be the same. Maybe we should have kept the van."

Angela shook her head and straightened away from him. "You wouldn't have been able to drive it through the cattle or off the road like you've driven the bike. You made the right call."

Buck dismounted. His legs were a little shaky, but they held up while he worked the kinks out of them and his backside. He figured it was like riding a horse—you built up calluses the more you rode.

Once he was steady on his feet, he pushed the bike behind thick bushes and unstrapped his gear bag and her backpack and carried them to the top of the rise. There, they could see the low structures of the small village. At the moment, they were nothing more than dark shadows on the horizon. At least they could watch from where they were without disturbing the inhabitants or alerting them to their presence.

Buck couldn't be certain the villagers would be quiet about them being there. If Koku's men had threatened them, they might expose any outsiders to prove their loyalty to the local warlord, rather than be cut down for hiding a potential enemy.

Angela followed Buck up the rise and dropped to the ground, wrapping her arms around her knees. "We didn't get very far, did we?"

"Far enough away from Abu Hanafi's village that hopefully he won't catch any flak."

"Do you think the people we treated will tell Koku's men we were there?" she asked.

"I doubt it." Buck dug in his gear bag, drew out a pocket-size package and unfolded the contents.

Angela lifted her head. "What's that?"

He shook out what appeared to be an aluminum sheet. "It's a Mylar thermal blanket. It's not cold enough to worry about heat loss, but it'll be nice to lie on something other than the dirt while we sleep."

He spread it on the ground, sat on one side and patted the space beside him. "We'll have to take shifts sleeping. I don't want some goat herder to wander by and report our location to Koku."

"Since I fell asleep on the back of the motorcycle—and how I did that, I'll never understand—I can take the first shift." Angela dropped down beside him.

"Deal. But first, we should eat something to keep up our strength. I have four packages of MREs. If we're smart about it, we can make them last for two to three meals each, between us."

"I have a couple of bottles of water and a twelve-pack of protein bars," Angela offered. "I wish I'd thought to bring more."

"We were in a little bit of a hurry getting out of

the refugee camp. I was surprised you got out with any of your medical gear." Buck pulled out an MRE package and tore it open, spilling the contents onto the blanket.

He opened the largest pouch and sniffed. "It's Italian food. I love the spaghetti and meatballs almost as much as the shredded barbecue." He glanced across to Angela. "We'd have to use precious water to heat the meal, or we can suffer and eat it cold. It's up to you. If we use the water, we can save it for the next meal in a marked bottle."

She shook her head. "I've eaten MREs. I can take them cold, when necessary. The point is to keep our bodies fueled." She took the plastic fork and the packet of food from him, stabbed a meatball and shoved it into her mouth. After chewing for a few moments, she gave him a weak smile. "See? Not bad."

He took the packet and ate the next one. He, too, was used to eating whatever he could, whenever he could, knowing it might be a long time before his next meal. The flavor of the marinara sauce was much more palatable when warm, but he couldn't feel bad about eating cold food. Plenty of people in the refugee camps went hungry for days before the aid trucks arrived. *If* they arrived, and weren't waylaid by ruthless thieves and warlords like Koku.

They finished the spaghetti and meatballs and saved the crackers and peanut butter for a snack later.

Angela dug in her backpack. "I have two bottles of water left."

"I have—" he glanced in his gear bag "—three, and my CamelBak is full."

"CamelBak?" she questioned.

"It's like a backpack you can fill with water. There's a straw you can use rather than pulling out a bottle or canteen. So you can drink on a march or run." He pulled a small pair of binoculars from the bag and handed them to Angela. "You might want to keep an eye on what's going on in the village. If anyone starts this way, wake me. We might have to make a run for it."

She took the binoculars and raised them to her eyes, staring out over the field to the village. "No one is awake yet," she said.

"Good." Buck stared at Angela in the starlight. "Are you sure you're up to standing watch on only a few minutes of sleep?"

"I'm awake. I might as well be useful." She continued to look through the binoculars. "Sleep. I'll wake you if I need you."

He lay back on the Mylar blanket and laced his hands behind his head. A long silence stretched between them.

Buck was good at taking whatever catnaps he could snag, whenever he could. Sleep was yet another way to fuel your body for the task ahead.

But Angela was sitting next to him, and her mere presence was keeping him awake. He wanted to reach out and touch her, as if to make sure she was real and not something made of his dreams.

This woman had haunted him from the moment he left Chicago to the moment he found her protesting in the streets of Bentiu.

He'd fallen in love with her when he witnessed her compassion toward other students, patients and anyone she came into contact with. She was everything the life he'd led in the gang was not. Angela was good and pure and out to help the world, not tear it apart.

Buck's chest tightened. He'd never stopped loving her, even when he was half a world away. But she'd been better off without him weighing her down. He'd had to believe that in order to leave the way he had. And seeing her again, the proof of her success and continued compassion only made him love her more.

ANGELA HAD BEEN sitting in silence, staring through the binoculars at the tiny village but not seeing a single hut through the lens. Her memories overlaid her vision with images of medical school, studying long hours with Buck and falling asleep in his arms on the couch in her apartment.

She'd given her heart to this man without holding anything back. And he'd left. No note. No explanation. Just left. How her heart had broken. She'd feared he'd been kidnapped or murdered when he hadn't shown up for class. Her calls went unanswered and his phone was finally disconnected. If she hadn't cornered his roommate and demanded to know what had happened to him, she wouldn't have known he'd dropped out of school and joined the navy.

Angela never understood. Why had he left her without a word? Why had he joined the navy? And he hadn't been around to give her any answers. Her eyes stung with a hint of the tears she'd shed for days back then. She'd had a hard time concentrating on her studies. The medical licensing exam had passed in a blur. How she'd passed, she hadn't a clue.

"I always knew you'd be a great doctor." Buck's whispered words jolted her back to the present.

"Quitting wasn't an option," she shot back automatically. After the pall of sadness lifted, she'd gone through an angry stage, much like the stages of grief. She'd wrapped herself in her anger, using it to push through her internship. No, she didn't take her anger out on her patients. She also didn't date, preferring to remain focused on her goal—to become a liccnsed physician and get the hell away from the place that reminded her of her first love.

"One question," she said. "Then you can sleep."

"Shoot."

"What happened with that gang...was that what made you leave?" She lowered the binoculars and turned toward him.

Buck lay with his eyes closed without responding.

At first Angela thought he might have fallen asleep.

But he finally opened his eyes and met her gaze. "I didn't tell you at the time, but I used to belong to that gang."

She frowned. "Those horrible people who nearly killed our classmate?"

He jackknifed to a sitting position and shoved a hand through his hair. "Those bastards who nearly killed you. Yes. I was a member of that gang when I was in high school and the summer after I graduated."

She shook her head. "I thought you knew them, but I didn't realize you were a member of their gang. I can't see you being that cruel."

He lay back down and stared up at the sky. "Yeah, I was a hoodlum. I never told you that part of my life. I didn't want you to think any less of me. The dirt on me is that my parents divorced when I was five. My mother worked two jobs to keep a roof over our heads and put food on the table. My father disappeared. He never paid child support, so it was up to my mother to handle everything." Buck glanced down at his hands. "She wasn't around much."

Angela reached out to touch his hand. "You never talked about her."

"She was so proud of me, going to college when she hadn't even finished high school." His jaw tightened. "She died of cancer the year I graduated with my bachelor's degree. She didn't even get to see her only son walk for his diploma."

"I'm sorry," Angela said.

"For what? You didn't give her the cancer."

"I'm sorry she didn't get to see you earn your degree and get accepted into medical school."

"Anyway, when I was in high school, I didn't have brothers and sisters to keep me company while my mother worked her two jobs, so I went out and found friends." He laughed, though there wasn't any humor in the sound.

"The gang?" Angela asked softly.

He nodded. "They accepted me for who I was. Or at least I thought they did. They really accepted me to become what they were—thieves, thugs and miscreants."

"Why didn't you tell me this when we first met?"

"I didn't tell you everything about my life before college. I didn't think it was relevant to who I was when I met you. I'd left that life behind when I went to college. I wasn't that person anymore."

"It was most certainly relevant. You are shaped by the events of your past and the people around you." She turned to fully face him. "You made a conscious decision to leave that way of life, and you were a better man for it."

He snorted. "It didn't keep the past from catching up to me."

"What do you mean? I thought they arrested the gang members."

"Some of them. But it didn't stick long enough. Their leader had a rule—once a member, always a member, until death."

Angela shivered in the warm morning air. "Is that why they came after us?"

Buck nodded. "I went to collcge in a small town, far enough away from Chicago that the gang didn't bother to come looking for me. But when I came back to Chicago for medical school, I knew I risked running into them. Even then, I'd been in medical school for a couple years without confrontation. So I got sloppy. I wasn't as vigilant. And then the chance encounter that night told them I was still around.

Their leader decided he needed to enforce his rules and make an example out of me."

"Couldn't you go to the police?" she asked.

"And tell them what? Until they actually hurt someone, I could do nothing."

"And then they did hurt our friend." Angela remembered arriving at their friend Brandon's apartment and finding him hurt and bleeding. And the gang being there, having set a trap to lure Buck to them.

Buck had fought hard. He'd wanted her to run, but the leader of the gang hit her, knocking her to the ground. That's when Buck had turned into a raving maniac and nearly killed every one of the gang members in Brandon's apartment.

Even the leader had suffered a broken nose and broken ribs from Buck's defense.

Angela had never seen Buck that crazed. But she'd thought it had all ended up well in the long run.

"I remember," Angela said. "The police hauled off the members of the gang, including their leader. They went to jail. We were so happy we didn't have to worry anymore. I thought it was all over." They'd celebrated in her bed, making love through the night.

"Our relief was short-lived. Their leader was out within a week," Buck said, his tone flat.

"So? Not all of them were out, were they? He was just one man."

"No, not all of them were released. But he wasn't going to forget that we caught him, and that he had to spend a week in jail. He was out for blood." Buck's jaw tightened. "Mine. And anyone who meant anything to me."

Angela's pulse leaped. "So you left?"

"I left to take away any reason they might have to hurt me. And I severed all ties so they wouldn't come after you or anyone else at the school."

Her throat tightened, and she had to swallow hard to force words past her vocal cords. "You could have told me."

"I couldn't. I turned off my phone and cut all ties to Chicago. If they wanted to hurt me, they'd have had to come to the naval training base to do it." Buck lay with his eyes closed, his face turned to the sky. "I did the only thing I knew would keep you safe— I got the hell out of your life."

Angela stared at his taut face. "You left to save me." She remembered how hurt she'd been, and she never wanted to feel that sad again. She'd turned her hurt into anger and worn it like a shield to guard her heart from ever being broken again.

How could she forget that lesson so quickly? He'd stormed back into her life, but he couldn't storm back into her heart. No. Just no. Her chest was tight at the memory. She couldn't go through that again.

Angela snorted, rebuilding the barriers that had helped her make it through those dark days after he'd left. "I don't buy it. You didn't even ask me if I wanted to go with you. That, to me, says you ran away from commitment. We were getting too close. You couldn't stand the heat, so you got out of the fire." She lifted the binoculars to her eyes. "I didn't ask you to save me, so don't give me that bullshit. Just go to sleep. We need to be rested for when we get back on the road tonight."

Angela resisted turning to study Buck's face for a reaction to her comments. The anger that had seen her through her residency was back and in fine form. She sure as hell had better hold onto it and keep it close like a shield, or she might fall into that pathetic habit of believing him again.

After all the years apart, after she'd congratulated herself on getting over this man, why did he have to come back into her life when she was doing just fine without him?

Chapter Five

"Buck." A voice called to him as if from a long distance away.

Buck had struggled to get to sleep after Angela had told him how she felt about him leaving her.

She had a right to be angry and to feel like he'd skipped out on commitment. He'd gone over and over his decision, wondering if she'd been right and he'd run from responsibility and from giving his heart to someone. His parents hadn't set the best example for handling relationships. What made him think he could make one last?

All those thoughts roiled through his mind as he lay with the sun in his eyes, trying to fall asleep. Eventually, he must have nodded off, though he felt as if he'd only slept for a few minutes when he was awakened by her soft voice.

A warm hand shook his shoulder. "Buck, wake up. We might have trouble."

In a fraction of a second, he went from completely out to on his feet, in a crouched fighting stance. "What's going on?"

Angela handed over the binoculars. "A truck full of what might be Koku's men just pulled into the village. They're rounding up all the people."

He stared through the lenses, adjusted to clarify and saw what Angela was talking about.

A group of about a dozen men wearing military-style black clothing and wielding rifles herded men, women and children into the center of the village.

One of the gunmen was shouting at the villagers. Even from the distance, Buck could hear the echo of his raised voice, though he couldn't understand what he was saying.

He was yelling at a man dressed in the white robes of a village elder. When he didn't get the response he evidently wanted, he hit the elder with the butt of his rifle.

The man fell to the ground and lay motionless.

Angela gasped. "Did he just kill that man?"

"I don't know." Buck counted all of the men and made a mental note as to their positions.

"We have to do something," Angela said. "We can't let them kill all those people."

"There are only two of us and a dozen of them."

"You have a rifle, don't you? Can't you shoot them?"

He frowned at her. "You're a doctor. What about the Hippocratic oath?"

"I didn't say *I'd* kill them, but you could." She pointed to the village. "They're taking the children."

Buck raised the binoculars to his eyes again. Just as Angela said, they were rounding up the young boys and loading them into the back of the truck.

"We have to stop them." Angela started down the knoll, her mouth set in a grim line. "If you aren't going to do something, then I am."

Buck hurried after her and grabbed her arm. "If you go down there and confront them, they'll shoot you."

"Better me than those little boys," she said, her voice choking on a sob. She tugged at her arm, trying to break free of his grip. "You saw what they did to Mustafa. How many of those kids won't make it back to their families?"

"I want to stop what Koku is doing as badly as you do, Angela. But charging into a situation where we're outnumbered will solve nothing. We'd be killed and my team will still not know where to find Koku."

Angela stopped struggling and looked up into his eyes, her own glassy with unshed tears. "How can people be so cruel?" she asked. "To children, for heaven's sake."

Buck pulled her back into the shadows of the trees and bushes and enveloped her in his arms. "Those men don't think the same way you do. To them, people are like cattle. Slaughtering them doesn't faze them in the least. Not everyone is as compassionate as you are." He held her close, stroking her hair, reveling in how good it felt to have her so near. All the while, he kept his gaze on what was going on in the village.

The good news was that no shots were fired. The elder was still lying on the ground when the truckload of soldiers and little boys pulled onto the road and headed south.

"The village elder got up," Buck said. "I think he's going to be okay."

"Thank goodness," Angela whispered against his chest. "That was going to be my next suggestion, to go to him and see if there was anything we could do to help."

"That would have exposed us. You know we can't let Koku know we're heading his way."

"I understand. But you know me. I couldn't stand by and do nothing."

Buck hugged her tighter. "At the very least, we know we're heading the right direction. Mustafa was pretty clear about his directions so far." He pulled away from Angela slightly, holding her at arm's length. "We'll free those boys. But we have to get Koku out of the picture, or he'll continue to terrorize villagers and steal children to man his army."

Angela nodded. "They were so young," she whispered. "I feel like I should have done something to stop them."

"You can't. Those men were Koku's men. Koku is giving the orders. We have to take him out to stop this insanity."

Her lips tightened. "Then let's find that bastard and put an end to his reign."

Buck chuckled. "That's my girl." Before he could think about what he was doing, he bent to sweep a gentle kiss across her lips.

Her eyes widened, but she didn't resist.

That little bit of a lip buss wasn't nearly enough, so he did it again. This time, he gathered her closer in his arms and cupped the back of her head. His mouth crushed hers in a kiss that he'd waited for since he left Chicago. Like someone who'd been stranded in the desert, he drank his fill of Angela.

She moved her hands from his chest to lace at the

back of his neck, and then she rose up on her toes to get even closer.

Buck traced the seam of her lips. When she opened to him, he swept in and claimed her tongue in a long, sensuous caress.

He'd missed her. Even before he'd made his decision to leave Chicago, he knew he would. All the years between, he'd never found another woman who'd made his heart pound so hard in his chest, or one who left him wishing for more.

When he finally raised his head for air, he stared down at her, his pulse still racing, his heart swelling against his ribs. "I missed you."

She looked up into his eyes, her dark eyes even darker with desire. Then her face changed, her lips thinned and she backed away. "You knew where to find me."

"I didn't think you'd ever want to see me again, especially after I'd left without a word of explanation."

She shrugged and turned away. "It doesn't matter. What we had is in the past. What we have now is a partnership that will last only as long as it takes to find Koku. After that, you can go back to your job in the navy, and I'll go back to..." She raised a hand. "Well, whatever I can do to help people."

Buck reached out to take her hand.

Angela stepped even farther away, shaking her head. "We shouldn't have kissed. Nothing will come of anything between you and me. We weren't meant to be together."

But he wanted something to come of them. Now that he'd found her again, he realized what had been missing in his life.

Her.

And he wanted her back. "Angela—"

"Please, Buck, let's just focus on the task. And unless we're leaving now to follow that truck, I want to get some sleep. I think we'll have a long night ahead of us."

Buck didn't push. He suspected the night ahead would be even longer than either of them could imagine. Being so close to Angela and unable to hold her would be the most difficult challenge he had to face.

On a brighter note, based on the way she'd responded to his kiss, she wasn't immune. Definitely scared to get involved, especially after the way he'd treated her…but not immune.

ANGELA COULD HAVE kicked herself. What had she been thinking to return Buck's kiss? When he'd left Chicago without a word, he'd proven he didn't trust her to understand the situation. He didn't care enough about her feelings to give her an explanation. The man had disappeared out of her life, only to show up again years later in South Sudan, of all places.

And just because he was back in her life now didn't mean he'd stay. He'd joined the navy to get away from his old life. Well, his old life had included her. He'd gotten away from his gang affiliation, and he'd gotten away from a relationship with her. Since he hadn't returned, she had to assume that all he'd felt for her was lust. She'd been the one who'd fallen hopelessly in love with her fellow classmate. In medical school, that was never good. The training was intense. Love had nearly derailed her studies.

She'd counted it off as young love and fought her depression to get on with her life, telling herself he hadn't been worth the tears she'd cried. In the back of her mind, and deep in her heart, she'd still mourned her loss. She'd read first love was always the hardest to get over.

Angela thought she'd done a pretty good job moving on and living without him. Throwing herself into completing her studies and internship had helped. She'd volunteered for additional shifts at the hospital and worked with clinics on the side to fill her time. Anything to keep from going back to an empty apartment, where she'd stare at the walls for hours and wish she wasn't so darned lonely.

She'd missed him terribly.

She stretched out on the Mylar blanket and turned her back to Buck. It helped a little. But she knew he was there, and she couldn't deny the desire she'd felt in that kiss.

Holy hell, she could easily slide right back into that trap again. Falling in love with a man who didn't return the same level of feelings was a no-win situation. She'd be better off focusing on the task ahead. Save the boys and get back to her work with Doctors Without Borders.

SHE MUST HAVE fallen asleep, because when she woke, the sun was on its way toward the horizon. The day had passed and night was approaching.

Angela sat up and looked around. Her gaze sought Buck. When she didn't find him, her pulse quickened and she pushed to her feet. Where could he have gone? Surely, he hadn't left her to head out on his own. He wouldn't do that, would he?

Angela descended the little hill to where they'd stashed the motorcycle and breathed a sigh. The bike was still wedged into the bushes. Buck couldn't be too far. She raised her head and peered over the bushes toward the village. A slight movement caught her attention. There. In the tall grass. A dark head popped up, barely above the seeded fronds waving in the wind.

She'd recognize the dark hair and the stealthy way he moved anywhere. The man was like a cat, all sinew and grace. He was working his way back toward her.

Her pulse slowed and her breathing returned to normal. In the back of her mind, she'd thought, *he left me once—he could do it again*. But like he'd said, he'd left her to save her from being targeted by his old gang. She believed him, but she couldn't let that soften her heart. Soft hearts were easily broken.

For now, she needed him to help stop Koku from hurting the people she'd come to help, and to keep her safe in the process. Yes, he'd left her in Chicago all those years ago, and in the back of her mind, she wasn't sure she trusted that he wouldn't do it again. She didn't think he would, but still, she prayed he wouldn't leave her alone in a foreign country. Even Buck couldn't be that cruel.

Her stomach rumbling, Angela hiked to the top of the knoll and dug out the crackers and peanut butter and a bottle of water. They'd have to be careful and ration their food to make it last. She had no idea how long it would take to get to Koku's camp. Mustafa had walked for ten days to make it home. On a motorcycle, traveling at night, they should be there in a lot less time. Maybe even as soon as early morning. They'd only driven for two hours the previous night, due to everything that had happened in Abu Hanafi's village.

Buck pushed his way through the bushes and emerged on the grassy knoll. "Ah, good, you're awake, and I see you cooked dinner." He winked. "What are we having, steak and baked potatoes?"

"Crackers à la peanut butter." Angela slathered peanut butter on one of the big crackers and handed it to Buck. "What were you doing?"

"I wanted to make sure none of Koku's men stayed behind in the village."

"And?"

"I'm happy to report only villagers remain."

Angela could imagine the mental state of the families. The women would be heartbroken about losing their sons. "Did you see the village elder?"

"He was sitting outside one of the huts. He seemed all right. But what concerned me was that someone came to visit while I was watching."

Angela's gaze met his. "A visitor?"

"From what I could tell by all the hand gesturing, he was from another village." Buck's jaw tightened. "I think Koku's men came through their village as well, and Koku's thugs weren't nearly as nice in the other village as they were here."

"What do you mean?"

"The man had been beaten and his clothes were bloody."

Angela's heart sank. "Should we go now and see if we can help?"

Buck shook his head. "Not until dark. Our mere presence in a village could be dangerous to the villagers."

"Sounds like even when we aren't there, the villagers are in danger." Her instinct was to immediately go to where her medical skills were needed. Waiting was killing her. But for Buck to get the coordinates he needed, they had to keep their current location as secret as possible. Koku couldn't know they were headed his direction. If he learned they were coming, he might end their journey before they could pass on the information the SEALs needed to eliminate one of the most ruthless warlords in South Sudan.

Resigning herself to waiting until dark, she spread the rest of the peanut butter over the second cracker. "Are we leaving as soon as it's dark?"

"As soon as the sun sets, we'll push the motorcycle past the village before we start the engine."

Angela bit into the cracker and peanut butter, surprised at how good it tasted. She was glad Buck was sitting beside her. He made her feel safer just by being there. His skills as a SEAL would prove useful in the night to come. She glanced at him from beneath her lashes.

Buck's gaze zeroed in on Angela's mouth as she chewed her cracker.

Heat rose up her throat and into her cheeks. Was he going to kiss her again? Even though she'd rebuffed him the last time, her heart still raced in anticipation of his lips meeting hers. Why was it so hard to resist this man?

Buck leaned forward. "Angela," he said softly and reached out his hand.

She blinked, her breath catching in her throat. She swayed toward him, her lips puckering.

He cupped her cheek in his palm and swept his thumb across her bottom lip. "You had peanut butter on your lip." He brought his thumb to his mouth and sucked the peanut butter off. Then he popped the last bite of his cracker into his mouth and chewed, a smile tugging at the corners of his mouth.

Angela sat back, her cheeks burning, her mouth dry. How could he be that close and not kiss her? She'd been halfway to him, caught in his trance.

What a fraud she was. She'd been the one to shut him down the last time they kissed. And here she was, practically salivating for another.

She jammed the last of the cracker and peanut butter into her mouth and nearly choked, trying to chew it. Somewhere between staring at Buck's lips and falling into his dreamy gaze, she'd lost her appetite. But she had to eat and conserve her strength. The next leg of their journey would be grueling and long. She needed energy and her wits about her. If not to fight off Koku's men, then to fight her own attraction to this man who'd stolen her heart once before.

After dusting the crumbs from her fingers and swiping her hand over her mouth to remove any debris there, she pushed to her feet. "The sun just set. We need to gather our belongings and be ready to go as soon as the residual light wanes."

Buck nodded, drank from one of the water bottles and handed it to her. "It's dry in this part of South Sudan. You need to keep hydrated."

She drank from the bottle, recapped it and stored it in her backpack. "I'm ready when you are."

He stood, folded the Mylar blanket to a small rectangle no bigger than a man's wallet and slid it into a pocket in his gear bag. "Ready."

They walked in silence down the little knoll to where Buck had stashed the motorcycle in the bushes. He pulled it out into the open and secured the bags to the back seat. "We'll have to swing wide of the village to avoid detection. Not all the villagers have gone to bed yet."

"Should we wait until they do?" she asked.

"I think we can get around them without being spotted. Are you game?"

She nodded, ready to see this mission through. "Let's do this."

Chapter Six

Buck pushed the motorcycle in a large circle around the tiny village, taking twice as long than if they'd gone down the road. They had to dodge bushes and trees, push through tall grass, and circumnavigate the outlying huts.

By the time they reached the road on the other side, Buck was ready to blow the dust off their clothes. He climbed aboard the motorcycle and waited while Angela slid on behind him.

Her thighs wrapped around his and she fit snugly against him.

His body heated immediately. The woman set his world on fire. Their kiss had resurrected all the old feelings he'd harbored since he'd met her in medical school. After all those years, he'd thought he'd be over his crush. What it proved to him was that Angela had been anything but a crush. He'd loved her deeply, to the very core of his being. And he still did.

Not a day went by, nor a night, that he didn't think of her and second-guess his decision to leave.

Could he have confronted the gang and told them to leave her alone?

No.

That would only have made them more determined to torment her, and in the process, torture him. No one left the gang on his own two feet. Until Buck. Thankfully, that world was well and truly behind him. The gang leader had gone to jail for murder. He wouldn't be getting out any time soon. In spite of that knowledge, Buck had no desire to return to Chicago. He'd thought he would eventually end up somewhere out west—Colorado, Wyoming or Montana. Someplace far enough away from Chicago where his past wouldn't come close to following him.

And maybe, just maybe, he'd apply to medical school again. He'd finish the course and become the doctor he'd always dreamed of being.

Assuming he made it back to the States. In the wilds of Africa, with a warlord to locate, he had a lot to do between now and retirement to start thinking along those lines.

"Are you going to start the engine?" Angela asked.

Pulling his head out of his thoughts, he started the motorcycle. The engine roared to life, the noise a sharp contrast to the peace and quiet of dusk.

"Hold on," he called out and twisted the throttle, shooting the motorcycle forward along the road toward Koku's camp. He had to keep his focus on the mission in order to protect Angela and see that she made it out of South Sudan alive.

Not long after they got underway, they came across another of the small villages Mustafa had told them about. They smelled it before they reached the outer edges. Smoke lingered in the air from the wreckage of several huts that had been burned to the ground.

Buck pulled off the road and into tall grass before he shut off the engine and listened.

Behind him, Angela removed her helmet.

The sound of a woman wailing carried all the way out of the village to their location.

"We have to help," Angela said.

A fire still burned in the center of the village. The people he could see silhouetted against the flames were moving bodies and laying them out in the firelight. There appeared to be a number of injured, and possibly even more dead. His fists clenched. Koku's work. The warlord had to be stopped.

"I have to help." Angela untied her backpack from the motorcycle seat and started toward the village.

Buck grabbed her arm. "What's to keep them from telling Koku we were there?"

"The same thing as with Abu Hanafi's village. If we help them, they will help us." She shook off his arm. "You don't have to come. But I can't stand by and do nothing."

Buck sighed. She wasn't going alone. "Give me a second to mark the spot in this grass, or we'll never find the motorcycle when we need to."

He moved the bike closer to a lone tree in the middle of the field and laid it on its side. Find the tree, and he'd find the motorcycle. He jogged back to where Angela stood, staring toward the fire. Taking her hand in his, he hurried with her into the village, wondering if he was making a terrible mistake and putting Angela into a lot more danger than he should.

Once they entered the village, Angela took charge and went to work doing what she did best—helping people.

At first the villagers were afraid of the strangers, but they soon realized she was a doctor, there to help.

She quickly triaged the injured and determined who needed the most immediate attention and who could wait. With Buck's help, she stitched wounds, treated burns and set bones. What Koku had done to these people was horrible.

From what Buck could gather, the villagers had refused to let him take their children. They'd fought to keep their sons. All that had bought them was torched buildings and six dead adults. One of the dead had been the village elder, and they had many more injuries than they could afford to deal with and still work to keep food on their tables.

Angela and Buck worked through the night, stitching cuts, bandaging wounds and setting broken bones. By the time morning light edged up the horizon, they had seen and treated all who needed help.

Buck was exhausted, but he could keep going. His BUD/S training had prepared him for long nights of grueling work and little sleep.

Angela was a different story. Dark circles shadowed her eyes. She packed what little was left of the medical supplies she'd grabbed on her way out of the refugee camp and her medical equipment into her backpack and met his gaze. "Are we leaving now?"

He nodded. "We need to. If Koku's people come back, we can't be here."

She sighed and lifted her backpack.

Buck took the bag from her and slung it over his shoulder.

The villagers gathered around them. Small children tugged at their clothes. An elderly man with stooped shoulders and weathered skin stepped forward and held out his hand to Angela. "Thank you for helping us."

"You saved us," said a woman with a sling fashioned out of a scrap of fabric. She reached out to touch Angela's arm with her good hand.

A little girl with a big lump on her forehead tugged at Angela's trousers. "Please, stay," she said, staring up at Buck and Angela with big brown-black eyes. She appeared to have been viciously hit or kicked in the head by one of Koku's thugs.

Buck's heart melted. He never understood how anyone could be cruel to children. He bent to get eye level with the girl. "Sorry, sweetheart, we can't."

Angela stared into the eyes of the elderly man. "You can't let Koku's men know we were here. It could be bad for us, but I'm more concerned about you and your people. If Koku finds out we were here and you didn't tell him, he could kill all of you."

He nodded, along with all the other adults. "We will keep your secret safe."

A shout rose up from somewhere behind Buck.

Everyone, from the young to the old, ducked low as if expecting bullets to fly toward them.

Buck spun to face a young man limping toward them, leaning heavily on a long stick. Dressed in the black outfit Koku's men wore, he had a rifle slung over his shoulder and a rag tied around his leg, blood oozing through the fabric.

Men, women and children gasped and cried out in fear, backing away from the man.

Buck pulled his handgun from beneath his jacket, ready to shoot the man if he made a move to fire on them.

Angela touched Buck's hand. "He's not here to shoot us."

"How do you know?" Buck asked, his hand steady, his gun aimed at the man's chest.

"He's injured." Angela started toward the man.

Buck reached out to snag her arm. "What if he's faking it?"

"Why would he?" Angela shook free of Buck's grip and hurried toward Koku's man.

Before she reached him, he stumbled and fell, landing in a heap in the dirt.

Buck ran forward, reaching him before Angela. He checked the man for other weapons and took his rifle, sliding it well out of reach. Finally, he checked for a pulse.

The man was alive, but weak.

"Help me roll him over," Angela said.

Together, they gently rolled the man onto his back.

Immediately, Buck could see the problem. The man had a wound on his leg and it was still bleeding. He'd probably lost a lot of blood.

"Good Lord, he can't be more than seventeen." Angela held out her hand. "I need scissors."

Buck slid her backpack from his shoulder and dug

inside for her kit of surgical equipment, found the scissors, and handed them over.

She quickly cut the trousers away from the guy's leg and spread the fabric wide.

He had a four-inch gash, all the way through the skin to the bone.

"Give me the bottle of water."

"It's the last one," Buck warned.

She held out her hand. She'd give her last scrap of food to someone in need. It was who she was.

He handed over the bottle. She filled a large syringe with the water and flushed the debris out of the wound.

Meanwhile, Buck dug out the suture line and a needle. Using an alcohol pad to sterilize the needle, he then threaded it and handed it to her.

As she stitched, he dabbed at the blood with a gauze pad, keeping the edges of the skin visible. Within a few minutes, Angela had the man's leg sewn together and the bleeding stopped. She applied a gauze pad to cover the wound and wrapped it tight enough to hold the pad in place.

Koku's thug groaned and blinked his eyes open.

"What's your name?" Angela asked.

"Kaleel," he muttered. He stared up at her and then around at the faces of the villagers. His eyes rounded and he tried to sit up.

Angela pressed a hand to his shoulder. "You need to lie still and let your body heal. You lost a lot of blood."

His gaze shot to his rifle, being held by one of the older men. "That is my gun."

The old man shook his head. "Not anymore."

Kaleel looked around at the angry villagers and lay back. "Why did you let me live?"

The old man's mouth pressed into a thin line. "You are lucky the good doctor reached you first, or you would not be alive now."

The teen stared up at Angela. "You should have killed me."

She smiled. "I'm a doctor. That's not what I do."

He rested his arm over his eyes, blocking out the glare from the rising sun. "If I do not return soon to Koku, I will be dead anyway."

"You need to let your leg rest," Angela said. "And your body needs to recover and regenerate the blood you lost."

The young man peeked from beneath his elbow at the villagers standing around.

"They won't hurt you," Angela said. She glanced around at the people and gave them a stern look. "This man is injured. You will leave him alone."

The women and older men glared at Kalecl.

Angela held gazes with the old man who seemed to have assumed the role of village elder.

Buck nearly laughed. Angela had the heart of an angel, but when she gave that look, she had people agreeing to anything she wanted.

Finally, the old man nodded. "Because of all you did for us, we will leave him alone. But if he tries to hurt anyone..."

Angela nodded. "Fair enough."

The elder glanced at the sun rising in the sky. "You need rest. You can stay in my home," he offered. "Until dark."

Angela frowned and glanced around at the village and its people. "We need to be moving on."

"Koku's men patrol the road passing through our village. You will be seen if you leave now."

Angela met Buck's gaze.

He made the decision. "We'll stay until dark. But we need someone to be on the lookout for Koku's men."

The new village elder nodded toward two women. "Samya and Nahla will be in charge. But we will keep watch while you sleep."

Buck dipped his head. "Thank you."

"I don't like that our being here puts these people in danger," Angela said.

"There's too much of a chance of running into

Koku's men in broad daylight," Buck said. "Besides, you need rest."

"I don't need rest," she said and then yawned.

Buck chuckled. "Right." He glanced toward the old man. "We would like to rest in your home. Thank you."

The old man dipped his head. "You are welcome."

"We need to move Kaleel out of the open," Angela said. "If Koku's men drive by and see him lying here, they might come and ask too many questions."

Buck bent and looped the younger man's arm over his shoulder. Then he scooped him up and carried him deeper into the village.

A woman stood in front of a hut, waving him toward the entrance. "In here."

Buck carried Kaleel into the hut and laid him on a mat on the floor. "You give this woman any trouble, and you'll have to answer to me," he warned the young man.

Kaleel shook his head. "I won't cause trouble," he promised.

Satisfied with the young man's answer, Buck straightened and left the hut. He didn't like being away from Angela for long.

Back out in the open, he found Angela standing with the new village elder outside a mud-and-stick building. She waved for him to join her.

When he did, she motioned toward the door of the hut. "Munawwar says we can sleep here. He says not to worry—he will have the entire village watching for Koku's men."

"I'll stay awake while you sleep," Buck said. "Go on. You need rest."

"Yes, I do need rest," Angela agreed. "And so do you."

Buck shook his head. "I can go days without sleep."

"Maybe so, but you aren't as effective and alert."

She had a point. And he was tired. But leaving their safety in the hands of the villagers...

"They'll watch." Angela grabbed his hand and led him through the door. "You need your sleep, too."

Munawwar's woman had arranged a neat pallet of straw covered with woven blankets on the floor of the hut.

Buck let Angela lead him to the pallet. He dropped her backpack to the ground and shed his jacket and the holster beneath.

Angela knelt on the blanket and then stretched out to lie on her side. "Pardon me while I go right to sleep," she said with a yawn. She laid her head in the crook of her arm and closed her eyes.

Buck smiled down at her. He drank in the sight

of Angela curled up on the pallet. He wanted to lie down with her, but he was afraid to let his guard down and trust others to keep watch for them.

But he couldn't resist. He lay down behind her, curled his body against hers and pulled her back to his front, resting his hand on her hip.

She scooted back, pressing herself even closer. "Thank you for helping."

"You're an amazing doctor," he said. "I'm happy for you." And he was proud of all she'd accomplished.

"You're every bit as good. I'm just sad you didn't finish," Angela whispered and yawned again.

Buck felt that pang of regret he always felt when he thought about all he'd given up. But holding Angela in his arms now was worth all of his sacrifices. Had he stayed in Chicago, his old gang might have killed her to prove a point to him. He couldn't regret that they hadn't had that chance.

"Buck?" Her voice was as soft as the warm air in the hut.

"Yes, Angela?"

She yawned before continuing. "Will we see each other again after all this?"

He wanted to say yes, but he hesitated. He was a navy SEAL, and she was a doctor with the Doctors

Without Borders organization. How often would they be on the same continent?

"We'll see," he finally said. "Sleep, sweetheart. We have a long way to go."

"Mmm," she murmured. "Buck?"

He chuckled softly. "Yes?"

"I love you." The words came out so quietly, he thought maybe he'd imagined them.

"What did you say?" He tipped his ear toward her, hoping that when she repeated herself, he'd catch the words this time.

Her breathing grew deeper and her body was limp against his. Angela had fallen asleep.

Buck's heart squeezed tightly in his chest. Surely he'd heard her wrong. How could she love him after all these years? Hell, he'd left her without a word. Seriously, he must be half-asleep himself. He laid his head down, fully intending to get up after a few minutes and go back outside to stand guard over her.

Before he could do that, he drifted into a deep sleep, dreaming about white picket fences and half a dozen children with dark hair and blue eyes, running around a yard with deep green grass and a sky so blue it almost hurt his eyes.

His heart was so full, he could hardly breathe. He knew it was only a dream, but he couldn't help wishing it was real.

"Mister! Doctor!" a voice cried.

A movement beside Angela made her jerk awake.

Buck was on his feet, gun in hand, heading for the door as it was flung open.

A young girl, around ten or eleven years old, stood there, her eyes wide, her breathing ragged.

"What's wrong?" Buck asked.

"Kaleel…" She drew in a breath and rushed on. "Kaleel left."

Angela pushed to her feet, blinking the sleep out of her eyes. "He shouldn't be moving about. How long ago?"

"I don't know. He was there, and then he wasn't," the girl admitted. "I was supposed to watch him." Her eyes filled with tears. "I was playing with my doll. I didn't know he left until he was already gone." She reached for Angela's hand. "I'm so sorry."

Angela shook her head. "It's okay." But she knew it wasn't. If Kaleel headed back to Koku's camp, he could tell Koku where they were. She looked to Buck.

He nodded. "We need to leave." He glanced at the watch on his wrist, his lips pressing into a thin line. "I can't believe we've been sleeping all day. It'll be dark soon."

"Then we should be ready to roll as soon as dusk

settles." Angela reached for her backpack, but Buck grabbed it first and looped it over his shoulder.

"You aren't leaving us, are you?" the girl asked, tears rolling down her dark cheeks. "This is all my fault. You would not be going if Kaleel had stayed."

"No, we should have left hours ago," Angela said. "Your people aren't safe as long as we are here."

"But you helped my family," she said. "You are good and kind. Not like Koku. He is evil. He took my brother Jamal. I miss my brother."

The old man whose house they'd slept in appeared behind the girl and laid a hand on her shoulder. "You cannot keep the doctor here. It is too dangerous."

The girl straightened her shoulders and wiped away the tears. "Yes. You must go. We would not want Koku to find you."

Angela didn't tell the old man and the girl they were searching for Koku's camp. To them, heading into Koku's camp would sound crazy. Why would anyone go near Koku if they had a choice?

As Angela and Buck left the hut and walked through the village, the sun sank below the horizon, casting the huts in deep shadows.

Children ran around their legs and the adults reached out to touch them as they passed, thanking them for all they had done to help their injured.

Angela smiled and squeezed several hands as she

worked her way through the throng of villagers to the edge of the town.

Dusk quickly turned into dark, and stars slowly began twinkling in the night sky.

Buck took her hand and guided her through the tall grass to the tree where he'd left the motorcycle. He strapped her backpack on top of his gear bag and pushed the bike toward the road.

She followed close behind. The stars had not quite lit the sky sufficiently for her to see where she was going. She tripped once but caught herself before she fell to the ground.

Buck paused and turned back. "You all right back there?"

"I am." She hurried to come up alongside him.

"Did you get enough sleep?" he asked.

"Yes, I did," she lied. She could have slept for an entire day and night; she'd been that exhausted.

"You needed it."

"And so did you," she said. "I'm glad you got some sleep as well."

"I should have stayed awake." Buck's voice was tight. Almost curt. "Kaleel could have snuck in and murdered us both in our sleep."

"But he didn't," she reminded him. "We helped him. He returned the favor."

"By not killing us?" Buck snorted. "He might well be on his way to Koku to report our whereabouts."

"Do you think he will?" Angela asked.

"If he's loyal to Koku, he will."

"I hope he doesn't. Not for our sakes, but for the sake of the villagers." Her chest tightened. "His people did enough damage without our visit being a factor. I can't imagine what they'll do if they know we've been there."

"Hopefully, they won't come back." He paused near the road and shook the motorcycle. "Sounds like we're getting low on fuel. We'll need to purchase gas soon. I doubt the villagers have gasoline."

"No. But Mustafa said there was a larger town after the two small villages. We should be able to find a gas station there."

"If we make it there," Buck said.

"Are we that low?"

Buck pulled out his small flashlight, twisted off the gas cap and shined the light down into the tank. "It's pretty low. We probably have enough to get us to the next town, but we'll have to fill up once we get there."

"How will we do that and not alert Koku?"

"If the town is big enough, we should be able to fly under his radar. At the very least, we should be able to get in and out before his people are notified."

Angela hoped so. She wasn't sure how much longer she could continue on. Riding a motorcycle impacted a different set of muscles than sitting in a car or standing as she examined patients. Her thighs ached from clamping around the seat and Buck's backside.

Buck started the engine and scooted forward so that Angela could slide her leg over and settle in behind him.

He twisted the throttle and sent the bike speeding toward Koku and the stolen boys.

Angela held on tight, wondering what the night held in store for them. No matter what, she had her arms around Buck, and that had to be enough for the moment.

THEY TRAVELED THROUGH the middle of the night, only slowing when they had to swing around a squatters' camp or a herd of cattle. Just when Angela thought her bottom couldn't get any sorer, they spied in the distance lights of what seemed like a newer town. As Mustafa had indicated, this was a larger settlement. It had more modern buildings made of brick and mortar, and it had electricity.

Buck pulled to the side of the road before they got too close to homes and buildings. "The gas stations likely won't open until daytime. We might as well find a place to park and catch some shut-eye."

Angela had been sitting so long, her legs had gotten stiff and her thighs were sore and achy. When she swung her leg off the seat, she nearly fell over.

Buck reached out and snagged her arm, yanking her up against him. He held her for a long moment, still sitting on the bike. "Are you okay?"

She nodded, her face pressed against his shirt, her fingers digging into him. He smelled of the wind and dust, but on him, it smelled earthy and good. Angela inhaled deeply, memorizing his scent, wishing she could be with him and smell him always.

As her legs acclimated to the standing position, she had no excuse to lean into the man, and he needed to get off the motorcycle and move his legs as well.

With a sigh, Angela straightened. "Thanks."

Buck swung his leg over the seat and stood beside her. "I should take you back to where it's safe. The closer we get to Koku, the more dangerous it will become."

"I want to find his camp as much as you. Those bastards are stealing children and killing villagers. They have to be stopped." She lifted her head to stare up into his eyes that were so dark, and yet, they shined in the starlight. "We have to find them. Then we can get your team in to take out Koku."

Buck cupped her cheek in his palm and brushed his thumb across her lips. "You're a brave woman."

She laughed. "Or just too stupid to know better."

"Never. You're also one of the smartest women I've ever known. And you always put others ahead of your own needs and safety."

She shook her head. "Which leads us back to *too dumb to know better*. And I get scared. How brave is that? Not very."

"No." He closed the distance between them and cupped her cheeks in both of his hands. "Courage is being scared but doing whatever needs to be done anyway." He bent, his lips hovering so close to hers she could practically taste them. "You're amazing."

Angela wanted that kiss so badly, she lifted up on her toes. When her lips touched his, every other thought left her head. She was where she wanted to be. In this man's arms, kissing him. Loving him like she always had.

His tongue traced the seam of her mouth.

She opened for him, meeting him with her own tongue, thrusting against his. Her hands circled the back of his neck, pulling him closer, her breasts rubbing against his chest, her hips pressing to his. The hard ridge of his desire nudged her belly, making her want so much more.

Lights blinked in the darkness, bringing her up out of the lust-filled coma she'd fallen into.

Buck's head shot up. His hands gripped her arms and he set her aside.

A vehicle rumbled toward them along the road, heading into the town. If they didn't want to be noticed, they had to get off the side of the road quickly and ditch the motorcycle.

"That's our cue." Buck grabbed the bike and started pushing it toward a stand of trees and bushes.

Angela followed.

Time to hide.

Chapter Seven

Buck found a little copse hidden in a stand of trees, surrounded by thick bushes and underbrush. He pushed the bike into the bushes and covered it with branches to keep anyone from seeing it from the road. They'd have to hunker down and wait until daylight, and maybe a little longer, before they could ride into town and put gas in the fuel tank.

The town appeared to be large enough that they might get away with acting like they were just another couple of crazy tourists riding a motorcycle on their way to South Africa.

If Angela left her helmet on, no one might even realize she was a woman until after they got their gas and got the heck out of town.

If he could get the pumps to work at night, he'd be willing to sneak in and steal the gas rather than put Angela at risk. But he wouldn't leave her alone. Not for a moment. Too much could happen in the short amount of time he'd be gone. She could be eaten by a lion, or nabbed by human traffickers. Or she could be captured by Koku himself. The man was ruthless. Buck didn't want to think of the horrible things he could do to Angela if he caught her.

Once they were tucked into the little copse, he spread the Mylar thermal blanket on the ground and laid his bag and her backpack down for her to use as a pillow. He pulled out a packet of MREs from his gear bag and handed it to Angela. Then he fished around in his bag some more and brought out his CamelBak and shook it. "I think we're still okay on water. But we'll need to find Koku soon, or we're going to be thirsty." He handed her the CamelBak and adjusted the straw. "Go ahead and drink. Maybe we can pick up some bottled water when we get fuel."

While Angela drank, Buck pulled out the satellite phone. "I need to check in with my team. They'll be worried." He hit the numbers and waited for Big Jake to answer.

"Damn it, Buck! Where have you been for the past couple days?" Big Jake didn't waste time getting to the point.

Buck chuckled. "Sorry, dude. We've been on the road, moving at night as much as we can." He told Big Jake about Mustafa, trading the van for the motorbike and the village Koku's men had ransacked, how they'd helped the villagers and then were confronted by Koku's wounded man, Kaleel.

"He probably ran back to Koku to tell them all about you two. Tell us where to land and we'll pick you up. It'll take us a couple hours to get to you from Djibouti. You'd have to lie low until we arrive."

Buck stared across at Angela where she sat in the little bit of light that made it through the trees. "Want to get out of here?" he asked her.

She glanced up, the whites of her eyes glowing in the darkness. "What do you mean?"

"I can have our guys pick us up now and forget finding Koku."

She shook her head. "No way."

"What did the doc say?" Big Jake wanted to know.

Angela reached up and grabbed the phone from Buck. "No. I'm not bugging out until we find Koku and stop him from hurting these people." She paused.

Buck could hear Big Jake talking but couldn't make out what he was saying.

"I'm okay," Angela said. "Yes, we have food and water. Yes, Buck's taking good care of me. I will. Thanks for asking." She handed the phone back to him. "He wants to talk to you."

Buck's heart swelled. The woman was tough and she would do the right thing, no matter how hard it was.

"Buck here."

"We think you need to get back here," Big Jake said.

"Yeah, but we haven't nailed the coordinates for Koku. As soon as we do, we'll be on the phone with you."

"Don't go all John Wayne on us and go in on your own."

"Not happening," Buck assured him. "The man has a small army working with him. I'm not that crazy."

"And don't go so long between calls," Big Jake said. "We were worried."

"I'll do a better job of communicating," Buck promised. "But for now, out here."

"Out here," Big Jake echoed.

Buck ended the call and stashed the phone in his gear bag. Then he settled on the blanket beside Angela, turned on his small flashlight and opened the bag with the MREs.

"What do we have tonight?"

"I don't know, but I could eat shoe leather at this point," Angela said. "Do you realize we haven't eaten in over twenty-four hours?"

His stomach rumbled to emphasize her words, and they both laughed.

"I promise you a steak dinner when we get to Djibouti," he said. "Well, maybe not steak, but definitely something other than MREs."

"It's a date."

A date. He hadn't had a date with her in years. What would it be like to take her to dinner and a movie? "I'd like to take you out on a real date when we get back to the States."

She paused in the process of tearing open a package of crackers. "How would that be possible? You work all over the world. I work in Africa."

"How long are you committed to Doctors Without Borders?"

"My commitment is up. I just stayed on. I can leave any time I want after giving them notice."

"What about your folks? Don't they miss you?" he asked.

She smiled. "They've been out here to visit me on a couple of occasions, and I've been back once since I've been here. They're happily retired and traveling the States in their motor home."

Buck could picture them. He'd met her parents when they'd come to visit her in Chicago. "Do they still have a place in Wisconsin?"

Angela shook her head. "They sold their house when they bought the motor home."

Buck's pulse beat faster. "I'm stationed out of Little Creek, Virginia, when I'm not deployed.

What about you? Where are you when you're not in Africa?"

She sighed. "I'm headed back to Denver when I'm done here. That's half a continent away from Virginia."

Sweet heaven. She'd ended up in Colorado, where he'd dreamed of living when he retired or got out of the navy. "I could fly out to see you."

She pulled the crackers out of their airtight foil package and sat staring at them. "Who are we kidding? You have your life and I have mine. We're not even the same people we were when we were in med school. What good would it do to try to see each other?"

Pain stabbed Buck in the heart. As much as he didn't want to hear the words, he knew she was right. They were two different people. He had his job as a navy SEAL and she was a doctor. He tore open a package of Mexican-style chicken stew, not at all interested in eating. "You're right. Once we're out of here, we have no reason to see each other. But I would like to treat you to a better meal back in Djibouti before you ship out to wherever you're going next."

Angela didn't say anything for a while, taking the time to spread peanut butter onto the crackers. "I just don't want to start something neither one of us is able to finish. It hurts too much, and…well… I can't go through that again. For now, can we just be friends?"

His chest tightened so much, Buck felt as if he was having a heart attack.

She just wanted to be friends. How could he be a friend when he wanted to hold her, kiss her and make love to her? "You got it," he said, trying to sound natural when his jaw was tight and he wanted to yell out how he really felt.

They ate in silence.

Buck didn't taste anything. Or rather, it all tasted like cardboard. But he shoved it down his throat. He had to keep up his strength to see this mission through. Then he'd be on to his next assignment, and she'd be on to hers.

When they were done, he packed away the trash in his bag and drank from the CamelBak. Then he sat like a lump beside her, wishing he could take her into his arms.

She had yet to lie down and go to sleep. Instead, she sat beside him, her arms wrapped around her knees, staring into the darkness. "It's the right thing to do, isn't it?" Angela whispered.

"If you say so," he answered, a little more harshly than he'd intended.

"We'd never see each other."

"Yeah," he agreed. "My work as a SEAL makes relationships difficult."

"But some people make them work?" she asked.

"Some of my buddies are in relationships. Some are married and have kids. Though I don't know how they do it."

Angela sat awhile longer in the darkness without saying anything.

Buck couldn't think of anything to say, either, when all he wanted was to do was beg her to give him another chance.

"You should sleep" was all he could push past his vocal cords.

"Yeah," she said, but she didn't move immediately. Finally, she lay down on her side, turning away from him.

Buck sat next to her. Close enough to touch her, but feeling as far away as if she were back in Chicago. He hurt so badly, he could barely breathe. Why did she have to show up during his mission? He'd resigned himself to life without her, imagining she'd married and had a couple of kids by now. But there she was, lying next to him, single, beautiful and everything he'd ever wanted in a woman.

And she wants to be friends.

ANGELA LAY AWAKE, trying to breathe softly, listening to Buck's every movement.

Be friends? What the hell had she been thinking when that had come out of her mouth? The last thing she wanted was to be just friends with Buck. Back in med school, he'd been the love of her life. Since seeing him again, she'd realized how much she still loved him. Hell, she'd never stopped loving him. How could she ask him to be just friends?

Because she never wanted to feel the way she'd felt when she discovered he'd left without telling her he was going. Without an explanation. Without saying goodbye. Even lying beside him, remembering the pain of those days, made her heart squeeze in her chest, and her breathing became more difficult. He'd broken her heart. Shattered it into tiny pieces she'd found difficult to reassemble.

He could do it again. And she didn't want that kind of pain again. But being just friends was really not an option. When he left Africa, that would be the end of their time together. She wouldn't see Buck again. She'd have to give notice to the Doctors Without Borders organization and maybe stay on for another two weeks or a month. But then what? She'd said she was heading back to Denver, where she'd worked before coming to Africa. But she didn't really have a job or an apartment waiting for her. She'd put all of her worldly goods into a storage unit when she'd left.

She'd always known Buck had loved Colorado and wanted to live there one day. Though she'd tried to tell herself she'd only gone to Denver because she'd been offered a job there, she'd really gone there because of Buck. Somewhere in the back of her mind, she'd hoped she would run into him.

Ha! Like that had happened in any of the years she'd worked there. So she'd given up and left to work in Africa. And of all places, she had to run into him here.

Fate played cruel tricks on her heart. But she couldn't give it away to him. No. She just couldn't.

Tears slipped from the corners of her eyes, and before she knew it, she was crying. She tried not to make a sound, but she must have sobbed loud enough to get Buck's attention.

"Hey." Buck rested a hand on her shoulder. "What's wrong?"

"Nothing," she said, her voice choked. Then she sniffed loudly and could have died of embarrassment.

"You're crying." He tugged, rolling her over onto her back. "Why?"

She couldn't tell him she was crying because of him. He couldn't know how much it had hurt to ask if they could be friends. She refused to open her heart to more hurt, even though it pained her to put up barriers between them. So she told him the only thing she could think of. "Because I'm hormonal."

"Is it that time of the month?" he asked.

"No."

"Then why are you hormonal?"

"I don't know. I'm just sad." She scrambled for a reason. "I guess talking about my folks, our old house and Wisconsin made me a little homesick."

"Oh, baby." He pulled her into his arms and held her close. "Don't cry. I can't stand it when you cry. It breaks my heart."

"I can't help it," she said and buried her face in his shirt. "I can't stop."

He brushed the hair off her forehead and pressed his lips there. "Please, don't cry."

She hiccuped and more tears slipped from the corners of her eyes. "Why do you have to be nice? I'm trying hard to hate you."

"Hate me?" He leaned back and stared down into her face.

She tried to read the expression in his eyes, but what little light made it through the leaves only shadowed his face and eyes.

"Why would you hate me?" he asked.

"Because it's the only way I can keep from falling in love with you all over again."

"And you don't want to do that, do you?" He brushed his thumb along her cheek and bent to kiss her forehead again, and then pressed his lips to her eyes, one at a time. "I told you I'd be your friend. Friends aren't supposed to hate each other. And friends aren't supposed to fall in love with each other." He traced a line from her cheek to her mouth, his thumb brushing her lips ever so lightly.

"I know." Angela's tears slowly dried, but her pulse sped. She kissed the pad of his thumb and pressed her body closer to his as he held her close.

"But friends can comfort each other and hold each other when we're down," he said, kissing the tip of her nose and finally brushing his lips across hers. "As a friend, I could kiss away your tears."

"Yes, you could," she whispered, her hands sliding up his chest as if they had minds of their own. She locked her fingers behind his neck and pulled him down to her.

"As a friend, I would be remiss if I didn't keep you in my arms through the night. It's scary where we are."

"Very scary," Angela said and she raised her face, capturing his lips with her own. "As a friend, will you keep me close?"

"I will."

"As a friend, will you comfort me when I'm sad?" She kissed him again.

"You bet," he whispered against her lips.

"As a friend, will you make love to me?" she asked, her voice fading to almost nothing.

"No."

Her heart stopped and her breath caught in her throat. She held it, waiting for his next words.

"I can't make love to you as a friend," he said. "But I can as a lover."

She let go of the breath on a sigh. "Then don't be my friend. Just for tonight."

"What if I don't want to be your friend for longer than that?"

"I can't make any promises," she said. "You hurt me once. I thought I hated you. The anger got me through medical school and my internship, but I realize it was more than hate. It was self-preservation. Tonight is all I can promise."

He hesitated a moment, his hand still on her cheek. Then he pressed his lips to hers. "Then tonight it is." He rolled her onto her back and kissed her like there would be no tomorrow.

And Angela gave back, desperate for one more night together. It had to be the last. She couldn't let him back into her heart.

But she was afraid she already had.

Chapter Eight

When Angela had asked him to just be friends, Buck's life seemed to crash in around him. Yeah, he deserved it. He'd hurt her all those years ago by leaving without explanation.

But now that he'd found her again, he hadn't wanted to repeat his disappearing act. This was the woman he'd fallen in love with and never stopped loving. She deserved better.

Her tears had torn a hole in his heart, and he couldn't keep himself from touching and holding her until she stopped crying. But embracing her had been his undoing.

If she'd told him to leave her alone, he would have found the strength to let go, but she hadn't. She'd curled into his side, wrapped her arms around his neck and pressed her lips to his in a kiss that shook his world.

She couldn't kiss him like that and not have feelings for him. It hurt his heart that she'd been crying. And the fact that she'd been crying because of him made it even worse.

He'd really thought she'd be better off without him. That's why he'd stayed away from her. She'd gone on with her life, become a doctor and was now saving lives with her skills.

And here she was, wanting him to make love to her for only a night? Holy hell, how could he do that and walk away? He wanted her for more than the night. He wanted her for the white picket fence, half a dozen kids and forever.

This was the woman he'd dreamed of since he'd met her. And he was going to make love to her under the stars of an African night.

Hell, what if she got pregnant?

That thought brought him to a screeching halt. He leaned up on his arms. "We can't do this."

"What?" She blinked up at him, her body going stiff beneath his. "Why?"

"No protection."

She laughed, the sound breathy. "In my backpack. Side pocket. I have at least a dozen."

"You packed medical supplies and condoms?"

She smiled and cupped his cheek in her hand. "I hand out condoms to the women who don't want more children to feed. They work with their husbands to get them to wear them."

He dug in the pocket she indicated and found a condom, just as she'd said. Placing it to the side, he settled in to show her how good it could be between them again. Perhaps if he rocked her world, he'd convince her to give them a second chance. The logistics of the relationship could work themselves out in the long run. He'd make it work, somehow.

Leaning over her, he stared down into her face. The light of the stars and the shadows of the leaves on the trees made her skin a dappled silvery blue. "You're even more beautiful than you were in medical school. And I thought you were pretty stunning then," he said and kissed one of her eyelids, still salty from her tears.

"We've been on the run for a few days. I have to be a mess."

"A beautiful mess," he said and kissed her other eyelid.

Angela ran her fingers through his short hair and tugged on his ears. "Shut up and kiss me."

"I like telling you—"

She leaned up and pressed her lips over his, thrusting her tongue past his teeth to caress his.

He shut up and did as he was told, laying her back against the blanket. He kissed her slowly, thoroughly, and would have gone on forever, but they had to breathe at some point. When he was forced to come up for air, he trailed a line of kisses along her cheek, across the line of her chin and down the length of her neck to the base, where her pulse beat fast and strong.

She ran her hands over his shoulders and down his back to tug the T-shirt from the waistband of his jeans. Her hands were warm against his skin and sent fire burning along his nerve endings and blood rushing to his groin.

He pushed her shirt up her torso and pulled it over her head. Then he grabbed the back of his shirt, yanked it over his head and tossed it to the side.

She laughed, the sound light and happy in the stillness of the night. Angela sat up and reached behind her back to unhook her bra.

Buck placed his hand over hers. "Let me."

She shifted her hands to his chest and ran her fingers over the muscles there while he unfastened her bra and slid the straps down her arms.

Her breasts spilled out into his palms and he held them, their warmth seeping into his fingers.

Buck breathed in deeply, trying to pace himself. If he wasn't careful, he'd climax before he got started. He was that excited by her and her body. Slowly, he circled her nipples with his thumbs, then he laid her back on the blanket and took one of her breasts in his mouth and pulled gently.

She arched her back, urging him to take more.

He did, sucking as much of the firm orb into his mouth as he could, tweaking the tip with his tongue.

Angela clasped the back of his head in her hand and pressed him closer.

He rolled the nipple between his teeth several times and then let go to move to the other breast. There he teased and tasted, flicked and nibbled until she was writhing beneath him.

A sense of urgency made him move downward, flicking and tonguing each of her ribs, darting into her belly button and lower to the waistband of her trousers.

She reached for the button, but he brushed her hand away and pushed the button loose himself.

With excruciating slowness, he eased the zipper down, parting the fabric as he went. He peeled the jeans and her panties over her hips and down her thighs, and finally past her ankles and feet.

She lay naked in the starlight, her body covered in the softly waving shadows of the leaves.

"Beautiful."

"As are you, but you aren't nearly as naked." She tugged at the button on his jeans.

He took charge and shed his clothing and boots

then lay down beside her on the Mylar blanket, the cool fabric doing nothing to chill his desire.

He traced a finger from her breast down her torso to the mound of fluff at the apex of her thighs.

Angela lifted her knees and let them fall to the sides, opening herself to him.

Buck slid between her legs and pushed her knees higher before he leaned over and pressed a kiss to her soft curls. Then he parted her folds with his thumbs and touched his tongue to the nubbin of flesh between.

Angela moaned and lifted her hips.

He took more, sucking her between his teeth, tonguing the bundle of nerves until she cried out and clutched the back of his head, her fingers digging into his scalp. Her body stiffened and then pulsed, her hips rocking again and again as she rode the wave of her release.

Several minutes later, she lowered her hips and tugged on his arms. "Please. Come inside me, now," she begged.

He crawled up her body, found the condom and tore open the packet.

Angela took it from him and sheathed him in seconds.

Then he lay down between her legs and pressed against her entrance. This was where he'd longed to be from the moment he'd found her in Bentiu. In her arms. In her life, and inside her body.

"Now," she urged. She grabbed his backside, her fingers digging into his buttocks, and guided him into her.

He thrust, long and deep, driving all the way into her, his shaft stretching her channel slickened with her juices.

Once he was all the way inside, he held steady, letting her adjust to his girth before he slid back out. He started slow, increasing his speed with each thrust, until he was powering in and out of her.

She dug her heels into the ground and raised her hips to meet each thrust with one of her own.

The heat of his release rushed through him, igniting his blood and nerve endings until he shot over the edge. He thrust one last time, burying himself deep inside Angela, dropping down on top of her, lying skin to skin until the last wave rippled through him. Then he rolled to his side, taking her with him. He wrapped his arms around her and held her close, smoothing his hand through her hair. "You are amazing."

"You're not so bad yourself," she said, her voice a soft murmur. She yawned into his chest and kissed his nipple. "Thank you."

He chuckled. "For what?"

"Thank you for being my friend," she said and fell asleep with her mouth against his skin.

Sleep was the last thing on Buck's mind. He'd just made love with the only woman he'd ever given a damn about, and she'd called him her friend.

Holy hell. He wanted to be her friend and so much more.

He had his work cut out for him if he wanted to bring her around to his way of thinking. But she was worth the effort…and then some.

Chapter Nine

Angela woke a few hours later, wrapped in nothing but strong arms and the cool of the morning air. She blinked her eyes open and looked up into Buck's wide-awake gaze.

"Did I fall asleep?" she asked.

He smiled down at her. "You did."

"And you didn't wake me to get dressed?" She snuggled closer and slipped her leg over his.

"I hated to disturb you. You seemed to need the sleep. Besides, I like you naked."

Angel's cheeks burned. "Did you sleep?"

He shook his head. "I kept watch."

"Thank you." She trailed her hand over his chest, loving the feel of his skin beneath her fingertips. "But you should have woken me sooner. I could have done guard duty while you got an hour or two of sleep."

"I'm used to little sleep." He smiled at her in

the gray light of morning. "Besides, I got to watch you snore."

"I don't snore," she said and pinched the tip of his little brown nipple.

"You do. But it was cute." He pressed a kiss to her forehead and another to the tip of her nose.

Her body came alive the more she rubbed it against his. She pushed him onto his back and climbed up on top of him, straddling his hips, happy to see and feel he was as excited as she was. "Where's that side pocket?" She leaned over and dug one of the condoms out of the backpack and tore open the packet.

"I thought we were only making love for one night?" he said.

She nodded toward the gray sky, the sun still well below the horizon. "The night is not over yet."

He chuckled and sucked in a breath as she rolled the protection over his hard shaft. Then he lifted her up and positioned her over him.

Angela sank down, taking him into her, loving the feel of him filling her to the limit. She closed her eyes and drew in a deep breath, letting it out slowly. Then she rose up on her knees and came back down, and did it again.

Buck gripped her buttocks and guided her up and down, settling into a tantalizing rhythm that set her core on fire and made her nipples pucker.

Before long, she was rising and falling faster and faster.

Then Buck lifted her off him and laid her down beside him. He came down over her, parted her legs and drove deep inside her, thrusting again and again until his body stiffened and he buried himself deep inside her.

Angela wrapped her legs around his waist and dug her heels into his buttocks, holding him as close as he could get until his shaft stopped pulsing and he collapsed against her.

Although breathing was difficult with all of his weight on top of her, Angela didn't mind. She could die like this, knowing she'd never been happier. But the sun rose above the horizon. Another day had begun, and they had to get back on the road.

Buck rose up on his hands and slipped free of her. He pressed a quick kiss to her lips and then got up. Standing in the early-morning light, his body bathed in golden hues, he could have been a Greek god.

He extended a hand to her.

Suddenly shy of her nakedness, she allowed him to pull her to her feet. When she started to reach for her clothes, he stopped her with a hand circling her waist. "Just so you know... I don't give a damn that the night has ended. I'm not ready for this to be over. I'm not ready to let you go."

Her cheeks heated and she opened her mouth to say—what? She didn't know, nor did she get a chance to speak.

Buck's mouth descended on hers, crushing her lips with the force of his kiss. His tongue slipped through her teeth and slid along hers in a long, sensuous caress that left her knees weak.

Angela clung to his shoulders long after he lifted his head, her gaze on his lips, wondering how he made her forget everything, including her words of the night before.

Just friends.

Ha! They could never be *just friends*. The passion between them was much too combustible, as evidenced by the night before.

But Angela couldn't bring herself to commit to him. He'd broken her heart once, and so completely that she wasn't sure she could live through it again.

When common sense finally returned and she opened her mouth to tell him they wouldn't be able to see each other again once they left Africa, she felt like it was too late. The timing wasn't right.

He bent to retrieve her clothing. He held her bra straps as she slid her arms through, then he turned her and fastened the back.

The more he helped her, the longer he stood before

her completely naked, his shaft jutting out in front of him, still hard and thick from making love to her.

"You know I can do this by myself," she said.

"I know, but this is more fun." He held her shirt over her head until she slipped her arms into the sleeves. Then he dragged it over her breasts and down her torso, his knuckles brushing her skin as he did.

A shiver of awareness rippled across her body, making her want to remove the shirt and bra and go for another round of lovemaking in the morning sunshine.

Instead, she took the jeans from his hands. "I'll do the rest." And she stepped out of his reach.

Buck shrugged and dressed himself quickly in his jeans and T-shirt. Before long, he was wearing his boots and his light jacket. He tossed her backpack onto the back of the bike and strapped it down.

Angela lifted his gear bag and his shoulder holster with the handgun tucked inside. "Aren't you going to tie down your bag and wear your pistol?"

Buck shook his head. "I have a bad feeling about going into town. If anything happens and we're jumped, I don't want them to find my weapons or the satellite phone. As far as anyone knows, we're just a couple of tourists stopping in to get fuel before we get back on the road."

"But that means we'll have to backtrack to retrieve your bag."

"True. We'll have to come back this way before circling back to head out of town the opposite direction. We don't want Koku to know we're moving south toward his camp."

Angela nodded. "I get it."

He handed her the helmet. "You'll need to tuck all of your hair up in the helmet and wear your T-shirt untucked and baggy. It's hard to hide the fact that you're a woman, but the longer they have to guess, the better our chances of getting gas and getting out of town before they become clued in."

She nodded and carried the helmet as they pushed through the bushes to exit the little copse.

Buck led the way. He pushed a branch to the side and paused before completely emerging from the underbrush.

Angela couldn't see anything past his big body. But when he stiffened, she touched his back. "What's wrong?"

"Shh," he whispered.

Angela's pulse kicked up a notch.

"We have company." Slowly, he backed into the brush and let the branch swing in front of him.

Angela glanced through the limbs and leaves and gasped.

Beneath a nearby tree lay a pride of lions, basking in the shade and cleaning themselves.

"Holy hell," she exclaimed quietly. "How do we get past them?"

"I suggest we wait until they move," Buck whispered. "I'd rather not antagonize them."

Out of morbid curiosity, she watched the lions stretched out in the sun, their tawny hair golden and shiny. She leaned through the branches, fascinated by the beauty of the animals.

Buck snagged her arm, holding her back from pushing through the brush and out into the open. "You can't go out there," he said, keeping his voice low.

"How long do you think they'll remain unaware of us?" Angela asked.

"I don't know. It could take them all day before they decide to move out. We could be here awhile."

Angela bit down hard on her bottom lip. She wanted to get this show on the road again. To do that, they'd have to get past the lions, with the motorcycle.

"We can wait a few minutes, but we really need to evaluate our alternatives and come up with a way to get past them. In a hurry."

"How are you at driving a motorcycle?" Buck asked.

"Never have." Angela narrowed her eyes. "Why?"

"I'd let you drive and risk me being mauled, but no way am I turning you loose on the bike when you've never operated one."

She smiled. "Probably not a good idea. With my luck, I'd fall over and be eaten."

"Most likely, they'll leave when the engine starts up, but we can't be certain. They could be conditioned to hearing vehicle engines, considering how close they are to the road and town."

"True." Angela shivered. "I've heard some lions have been known to steal children from their beds at night."

Buck circled her waist with his arm. "We're armed and ready if they decide we look like lunch." He glanced around. "I just wish we could get to the bike without drawing their attention."

They'd parked the motorcycle in the bushes outside the little copse of trees before entering their own little grotto the previous night.

"Can we get to it from this side?" Angela whispered.

"We can try, but there are quite a few bushes in the way."

They moved slowly away from the lions and back into the tiny grove.

Buck carefully moved aside branches and leaves in an attempt to get to the motorcycle.

Angela held back limbs and helped where she could, but the brush was thick. Getting a man through was one thing. Getting a man and a motorcycle through…well, it didn't look promising. She tried to keep an eye on the pride, but she couldn't see through the branches to know what was going on with them. They seemed so big and lazy. Surely they wouldn't see her and Buck as a threat.

Between Angela and Buck, they eased the motorcycle through the thick brush into the tiny clearing. Buck quickly strapped Angela's backpack to the seat and hung his gear bag up on a branch, hopefully out of reach of the lions.

"Why aren't we taking yours?"

"I hate leaving it, but if we're caught in town with a bag containing a military-grade weapon, we might not make it back out."

"What about the satellite phone?" Angela asked.

"Another item I don't want someone finding on us. I think we could explain it, but if we're robbed, I'd rather not have it taken." Buck adjusted the bag so that the tree branch it rested on hid it from sight. "We'll come back here as soon as we can."

"You mean, as soon as the lions leave," Angela said.

"Yes, and as soon as we fill the gas tank and ditch

anyone following us. I'd rather they thought we were heading back north, anyway."

Angela stared at the bag. "I don't like leaving the satellite phone."

"Me either, but I don't want anyone taking it from us. Plus, I don't think anyone will find it. Especially if the lions stay here much longer." He glanced around the small clearing. "I'd almost rather leave you here while I go into town for the fuel."

She shook her head before he finished speaking. "You're not leaving me anywhere."

He kissed her forehead. "You're right. I don't trust the animals around here. Two or four legged." He handed her the helmet. "Put this on and tuck your hair up inside. The less obvious it is that you're female, the better."

"I'll just be a boy on the back of your bike." She untucked her shirt and stretched it enough that it would hide her curves.

"Sweetheart, even making your shirt baggy can't hide that you're a woman." He pulled her close and hugged her to him. "Just stay with me. I don't want anything to happen to you."

"I'll be like a fly on flypaper," she said with a grin. "Like white on rice. Like stripes on a zebra, like—"

Buck chuckled softly and pulled Angela into his

arms. "You're an amazing woman. I repeat, I'm not giving up on you, so expect a fight." He crushed her lips with his.

Buck kissed Angela until her toes curled and she forgot all about the lions lurking on the other side of the bushes. When he raised his head, he chucked her beneath the chin and winked. "Now, let's run the gauntlet of lions. We'll be going fast, so you'd better hold on tight."

Angela had barely caught her breath from the kiss when she slid onto the back of the motorcycle. "How are we getting out of here?"

He nodded toward a break in the bushes on the opposite side from the lions' lounging location. "We're going through there at top speed. Keep your head down, your helmet buckled and your arms around me. It's going to be a bumpy ride."

After a quick glance at the lion pride, she nodded. "They're still pretty calm."

"Let's hope they stay that way." Buck swung his leg over the seat and moved forward.

Angela slid on behind him.

"I don't like you riding on the back. If the lions come after us, they'll get you first."

"Then we'll just have to ride like the wind." Angela wrapped her arms around his waist, sucked in a deep breath and held it while Buck turned the key.

The engine rumbled to life. "Ready?" he shouted.

"Go!" Angela yelled.

Buck twisted the throttle, launching the motorcycle forward and through the branches.

Angela ducked her head and pressed it, helmet and all, into Buck's back. Branches and thin tree limbs whipped at their heads, necks, arms and legs as they blew through the barrier and out into the open.

Buck swung wide of the lion pride, circling back to the road heading into the town.

Daring to turn back, Angela spotted three lionesses running toward them. "Go! Go! Go!" she yelled.

Buck gave the engine more gas and sped toward the town.

The lionesses raced after them, gaining ground.

Buck shot forward at full throttle, building up speed and flying over the uneven ground.

Angela held on until her arms ached. The bumps were so bad, they nearly threw her from her seat. She clamped her legs around Buck and locked her hands and wrists around his belly. If she came off the bike, she'd take him with her.

Soon, they were going so fast even the lionesses couldn't keep up. They slowed to a walk and turned back toward the pride.

Buck slowed their mad pace as they connected with the dirt road and headed into the town.

Angela couldn't help but think they were going from one lion's den into another. She prayed they didn't run into danger. This man she was holding onto for dear life meant more to her than he could possibly know. She didn't want him to die protecting her. And she was seriously considering retracting her "just friends" requirement for their relationship. She wanted the chance to tell him that when this was all said and done.

BUCK COULDN'T HAVE left Angela in the stand of trees, or he would have. Surrounded by lions, she wouldn't have been any safer than riding with him into a town that could well be occupied by Koku's men. His gut was telling him this was a bad idea, but the gas tank was telling him he was out of choices.

They had to have fuel, and this was the closest town with the potential to have a gas station.

He drew in a deep breath and drove into the outskirts of shacks and huts that gradually transformed into concrete block buildings. Before they'd gone more than a tenth of a mile into the town, a man in a long white robe stepped into the street and waved them down.

Buck's first inclination was to race past him, but

then he noticed the gentleman wasn't dark-skinned like most of the people of the Sudan. He was white and he had a gray beard. And he appeared to be frantic.

"Slow down. I think he needs help," Angela said.

More interested in getting fuel, Buck slowed to a stop next to the man, his hand going to the pistol beneath his jacket, only it wasn't there. He'd left it in the gear bag back in the copse of trees outside of town.

"Do you speak English?" the man asked.

"We do," Angela responded. "Are you in trouble?"

The man gave a hint of a smile and shook his head. "No, but you two are. You need to get inside quickly."

Buck stared around at the suspiciously empty streets. "Why?"

"They're on the other side of town, heading this way." The man stepped back. "Hurry!" He waved toward a whitewashed stucco building. "Get inside and bring the motorcycle, too."

A white woman in a blue dress similar to what the locals wore opened the door and waved them forward. "Hurry!" she said.

"I don't understand," Buck said.

The man gripped the handle on one side of the motorcycle. "I'm a Christian minister. My wife and

I are missionaries. Our parishioners warn us when the local warlord's men are on their way through. We hide until they're gone."

"We should go with them." Angela climbed off the back of the bike. "Even if we were willing to risk it, we might put these good people at risk."

Buck nodded and pushed the motorcycle toward the building.

"Take the bike around the back. I have a place in the shed where we can hide it," the preacher said.

His wife came out, hooked Angela's arm and led her toward the house.

Buck didn't like that they were being separated. "She stays with me."

The minister grabbed the handle of the motorcycle and urged Buck to roll it forward. "You'll only be apart long enough to stow the motorcycle. Longer if we stand around arguing."

Buck hurriedly followed the man to the shed behind the building. Calling the structure a shed was being generous. It looked more like a shack constructed of bits and pieces of lumber, plywood and tin. But there was a place to push the bike into the back behind what was left of an old truck that had been cannibalized for parts. Buck parked it beside the truck body, pulled a sheet of old tin next to it and leaned it toward the truck. If someone casually peered into the shed, he wouldn't see the bike, just the body of a rusted truck and a sheet of tin.

Once he had the bike in place, he grabbed Angela's backpack and carried it to the back door of the house.

The minister opened the door for him and closed it once he was inside, sliding a wooden bar in place to lock people out.

Buck walked through to the front room, where he found Angela and the older woman.

The minister held out his hand. "Let me introduce myself. I'm Hiram Woodby, and this is my wife, Gladys."

Buck shook the man's hand and nodded toward his wife. "I'm Buck and this is Angela—"

"His fiancée." Angela stuck out her hand. "I was just telling Mrs. Woodby about our exciting trip through the Sudan on motorcycle. We never expected to run into trouble along the way." Angela met his gaze and held it.

Fiancée, huh? Why would she want to keep secrets from the minister and his wife? But then, the less they knew, the less someone could torture out of them.

"Right, we were on a self-guided tour of Africa, hoping to drive all the way to South Africa."

The minister shook his head. "You don't realize

how very dangerous it is to travel the length of Africa. There are too many warlords, rebels and pirates around to make it through safely."

Mrs. Woodby wrung her hands. "You two really need to head back north. This area is not stable. Not at all."

Her husband waved toward several cushions on the floor. "Please, have a seat. We will wait until it is safe to go outdoors again."

"How long will that be?" Buck asked.

"Sometimes thirty minutes, sometimes longer," Woodby said.

"We'd like to head back north, but we can't until we get fuel for the bike," Angela said. "We were hoping to find some in this town. There are gas stations, aren't there?"

Mrs. Woodby shot a glance at her husband.

He reached for her hand. "There is one. But it's not safe to go there until the men have passed through."

"What men are you talking about?" Buck asked, hoping the minister could shed more light on the whereabouts of Koku's camp.

Angela sat on one of the cushions and patted the one beside her. "Sit."

Buck's lips quirked at the command, but he complied.

The Woodbys sat as well.

"As you might know, we're in predominantly Muslim territory," Mr. Woodby said. "The local warlord, Koku, doesn't appreciate our culture and would rather we depart the area. But we can't leave the people who've come to rely on us. So, they help hide us and we lie low to keep them from being punished." The minister squeezed his wife's hand and let go. "We should leave, but we don't have family waiting for us back in the States, or anyone who truly needs us more than the people here."

"Yes, the people here need us much more," his wife added. "So we chose to stay, even though we are in grave danger."

"This Koku...is he nearby?"

"He can't be too far, because his men come through often and rough up the locals, stealing food and fuel." Woodby's lips thinned.

Mrs. Woodby leaned closer and lowered her voice. "They've even stolen boys. We think they are training them to be in their evil army." She looked down at her hands. "We prayed they wouldn't, but they did. The mothers were beside themselves. Those poor children must be terrified. They were so young."

Angela reached out and patted the woman's wrinkled hands. "That's terrible. This Koku must be a monster."

"Yes, he is," Mrs. Woodby said. "So, you see, you

can't stay long. If Koku's men know you're here, they'll come after you."

"How do you know?" Buck asked.

The minister took his wife's hand again. "There was a Baptist preacher who came to town a couple of weeks ago. Koku's men came through and we haven't seen him since."

"We think they might have killed him." Mrs. Woodby's voice trailed off. "He was such a nice young man. So full of hope and good intentions."

"He didn't understand how dangerous it was here. He thought he could change how things are." The minister straightened his shoulders. "I would offer you the fuel you need, but we don't have any to spare. I could ask one of our people to get it for you."

Buck shook his head. "I don't want to put anyone in danger. If all we need to do is wait for Koku's men to leave town, we can wait."

Mrs. Woodby released a long breath. "Good. No use going out into the streets now." She rose from her cushion. "Could I get you some tea? We boil the water to purify it."

"Yes, please," Angela said.

Buck stood when Mrs. Woodby did. He waited until she'd left the room and then crossed to a window that had been boarded up from the inside and peered through the slats.

At first, he saw no movement. The streets appeared to be completely empty.

But as he continued to study the road, a truck rumbled past. In the front were two black-garbed men carrying Russian-made AK-47 rifles. When the truck passed, Buck counted half a dozen similarly garbed and equipped men in the back.

Buck's pulse sped. He fought the urge to back away from the window. The men in the truck couldn't possibly see into the home with the boarded windows. But they were close. Too close for Buck to feel comfortable.

The vehicle stopped in the middle of the road, and the men jumped to the ground. Moments later, they pounded on the door of the building across the street from the Woodbys' house.

When no one answered, the men kicked the door in and rushed inside.

"How often are they breaking down doors and entering homes?" Buck asked.

"Every day." Mr. Woodby came to stand beside Buck. "At first, they just harassed the townspeople. When they grew bored of that, they would drag people out into the street, beat them and then shoot them."

"For no reason at all," Mrs. Woodby added, re-entering the room with a tray filled with cups, saucers and a teapot.

The men emerged from the home across the street, empty-handed. The one who seemed to be in charge pointed to the house across from where he stood. The house was the missionaries'.

Buck's pulse leaped. "We have trouble."

The minister moved faster than Buck would have thought possible. "Gladys, take our guests into the secret room. And hurry."

"Yes, dear." Gladys set the tea tray she'd been carrying on the coffee table and turned away from the living area. "Follow me, please," she said.

"Yes, ma'am," Buck said.

She walked to a wall and touched the center and the wall slid open, revealing a staircase going down into the ground below.

"Come with me," Mrs. Woodby said, her tone short, clipped. The older woman went first, followed by Angela and then Buck. He didn't like leaving Mr. Woodby alone. If Koku's men kicked in the door, the man had no protection.

Halfway down the stairs, Buck stopped. "You two go on without me. I'm going to stay with Mr. Woodby."

"He knows what to do and say," Mrs. Woodby said. "If you're there, he'll be in more danger. Koku's men know he's here. For the most part, they leave us alone."

"I'll stay out of sight. But I don't like that he's alone and defenseless."

"He'll be in the Lord's hands," Mrs. Woodby said.

And if he were killed, Mrs. Woodby would be alone in a hostile town. She'd have a hell of a time getting out of South Sudan on her own.

"Don't worry," Buck said. "I'll be as quiet as a church mouse."

Mrs. Woodby stared at him for a moment and then nodded. "Okay. But do be careful."

Loud banging sounded on the door.

Buck ran up the stairs and closed the hidden door, hiding the women below. He hurried toward the front room and slid into the pantry cabinet with barely enough room for him to close the door.

And he waited.

Chapter Ten

Buck could see through the gap into the living room where the minister was opening the door for Koku's men.

No sooner had he removed the bar covering the door than the men burst into the room, nearly knocking down the old man.

Buck clenched his fists, his first instinct to go to the man's aid, but his wife's words echoed in his head. Just his being there would be more dangerous for the minister.

Hopefully, the thugs wouldn't rough up Woodby any more than they already had.

"Why are you still here, old man?" the leader demanded.

In a calm, even tone, Woodby replied, "This is my home."

"You are not welcome in my country. Take your

beliefs and your white man's ways back to where you came from."

Woodby dipped his head without replying.

Koku's man narrowed his eyes and glanced past Woodby's shoulder. "Are you hiding anyone?" He waved his weapon in the man's face. "If you are, we will kill them and you."

Woodby waved a hand toward the interior of the house. "You are welcome to search."

Buck cursed silently. Woodby didn't know he'd chosen to come back out of the basement hiding place. If the men found him in the pantry, they would attempt to kill him and the minister.

He braced himself for a fight.

The leader had stepped past Woodby and started toward the kitchen when a shout sounded from the street outside.

Buck held his breath, ready to spring if he needed to. The element of surprise was on his side, but he'd still be outnumbered and put Woodby in danger.

He held his course and waited to see what Koku's men would do.

Another shout sounded in the street. The man who'd confronted the minister spun and ran to the door. He yelled at the man in the street. "What?"

The man outside yelled back, his voice muffled by the walls of the building and the cabinet door.

Suddenly all of Koku's men departed the small home.

Woodby closed the door softly and slid the bar in place. He turned, leaned against the door and pressed a hand to his chest. Then he walked to the window and watched through the slats.

Buck left the cabinet and joined the minister. "Are you all right?"

The man nodded. "Shaken, but not hurt." He continued to watch the man outside. "You risked a lot by coming back upstairs."

"I know. But I couldn't leave you to handle those men. They might have gotten more violent."

Woodby shrugged. "It's part of my life. I trust the Lord to take care of me."

Buck hoped the Lord did take care of the man. He also believed the Lord helped those who helped themselves.

"They're moving on," the minister said.

"How often do they come in and do shakedowns?" Buck asked.

"More than we care for." The old man glanced out the window again. "Sometimes they just rough people up. At other times, they have been trigger-happy and shot residents." His lips thinned. "They're ruthless and godless."

Buck shook his head. "That doesn't bode well for you and your wife."

"No. But it also doesn't bode well for our parishioners."

"You have the choice to leave," Buck reminded him.

"And our people do not have that choice." The minister faced Buck. "My wife and I agreed to stay. We couldn't abandon them in their time of need." He crossed the living around and pushed on the wall, exposing the hidden doorway and the staircase leading down into the basement. "You can come up now."

Buck peered down the darkened stairway.

Angela was the first to appear. "Are they gone?"

Mrs. Woodby stepped up behind her.

"They're gone," Buck replied.

Angela stepped aside and allowed Mrs. Woodby to go up first.

When the older woman arrived at the top, she hugged her husband. "Why do they have to be so hateful?" she whispered and pressed her face into his chest. "I worry about you."

The minister stroked his wife's gray hair. "It's God's will."

"I wish God's will was to stop their reign of terror," Mrs. Woodby said.

"He will. He will," her husband assured her.

Angela stepped around the older couple and into Buck's arms. "I didn't like having you out of my sight." She held him tight. "I have to admit, I like having you around. I feel safer."

He smoothed the hair out of her face and pressed a kiss to her forehead. "I like knowing you're safe."

"You're welcome to stay as long as you like," Mrs. Woodby offered. "We can lay out a pallet on the floor in here for you two to sleep on. There's enough food in the pantry to feed us all for several days."

Buck stared down at Angela. "We can't."

She nodded. "We have to get moving."

They had to find Koku and get the coordinates to his team. The sooner they did, the better off everyone in the region would be.

Buck kissed Angela hard on the lips and stepped away. "I'm going out to get the fuel we need."

"I'm going with you," Angela said.

Buck hardened his jaw and his heart. "No. I need to know you're safe. I want you to stay here. You have a place to hide if Koku's men return."

"You said yourself you didn't like me out of your sight."

"I did. But if you're with me, I might lose focus

and get us both hurt." He lifted her hand, pressed a kiss into her palm and curled her fingers around it. "Please, promise me you'll stay."

Angela stared into his eyes, her own suspiciously bright. "I'll stay, but don't be too long."

He gave her a tight smile. "I'll be back as soon as possible."

"I'm coming with you," Mr. Woodby said. "I have a gas can in the shed. We can take it instead of taking the motorcycle."

"I'd rather take the motorcycle. I need to fill it to full, if possible."

The minister shrugged. "Either way, I can show you the way to the station by taking the back streets."

The man had a point. "The station should be on a main road, right?"

"Yes, but not all of the secondary streets run straight through. You could run into a dead end getting there and back."

"Let my husband help," Mrs. Woodby implored. "If nothing else, the people of the town know him and will help you sooner than they'd help a stranger."

"Any sign of trouble—" Angela started.

Buck nodded. "Any sign of trouble and we'll find a place to hide until it blows over." He grabbed Angela's helmet and handed it to the minister. "You'll have to use this."

Mr. Woodby grinned. "I always wanted to ride a motorcycle. The closest I've come is riding on a scooter. This will be a treat." He kissed his wife and led the way through the back of the house to the shed.

Buck followed, keeping a close watch on the corners of the building, listening for sounds indicating a return of Koku's men.

Once they had the motorcycle out of the shed, Buck mounted and waited for the minister to climb onto the back.

He started the engine and revved the throttle before easing out onto the main street running through town.

The roads were still fairly empty, with only a few men daring to get out after Koku's troops had come through.

Buck drove the motorcycle through town, coming to a halt at a building the minister assured him was the gas station. It had one old-fashioned pump Buck had only seen the likes of in photographs. He stopped the motorcycle at the pump. "It might be best if you keep your helmet on. I don't want people to know who is with me."

The minister agreed and kept the helmet buckled. He went into the building and addressed the man who owned the station. When he returned, he nodded toward the pump handle. "It's all taken care of.

Fill your tank, but make it as quick as possible. Fahd is afraid Koku's men will be back through soon."

Buck plugged the nozzle into the tank and pressed the lever. The gas poured into the tank so slowly, he gritted his teeth and prayed he could get what he needed in this century.

He didn't like being away from Angela so long. Anything could happen. Koku could return to the house and kick the door in. The women would be defenseless.

The more he thought about it, the more frustrated he became at how slowly the pump was filling his tank. When it was only half-full, he gave up, stopped the pump and hung up the nozzle.

"Hey!" someone shouted behind him.

He turned to see the leader of the thugs who'd burst into the Woodbys' home earlier, surrounded by six of his buddies, all carrying AK-47 assault rifles and wearing the black outfits of Koku's shoddy army. They were young men looking for trouble.

Buck didn't have time to put up with them. He wanted to get back to Angela and get the hell out of town. But if trouble was what they were looking for...well, they'd found it.

"Mr. Woodby, go inside the building."

"I'm not leaving you to these men."

Buck purposely replaced the cap on the gas tank,

ignoring the men heading his way, while keeping an eye on them in his peripheral vision. "Mr. Woodby, I need you to go inside the building and lock the door."

"But—"

"Now," he said, his tone low, brooking no further argument.

The minister hurried into the building and closed the door just as the thugs reached Buck and the motorcycle.

He glanced up and smiled. "Can I help you?"

"Yes, you can. You can give us your motorcycle."

Buck shook his head, the smile still in place, though forced.

"You want my bike? Come and get it."

ANGELA PACED THE FLOOR, wishing she'd gone with Buck instead of staying at the house, wondering what was happening on the streets of the town.

All sorts of scenarios rolled through her mind, none of them good. Had Buck and the minister run into Koku's men? Had the people of the town turned on them? Had they been shot by a sniper perched on a rooftop? The more she thought of all that could have happened, the faster she paced.

"Come. Sit. You're wearing a hole in the floor," Mrs. Woodby said. "I can warm up the tea I made earlier, and we can have some cookies I made out of the last of my flour and sugar."

"Thank you, Mrs. Woodby, but I'm not thirsty or hungry." She just wanted Buck to get back and show her he was fine.

The older woman stepped in front of her and touched her arm. "They'll be okay. You'll see."

The woman's soft smile and words of reassurance were just enough to send Angela over the edge. Tears pooled in her eyes and her lip trembled. "I'm worried about them. About him."

Mrs. Woodby opened her arms. "Come here."

Angela stepped into the older woman's embrace and laid her head on her shoulder, tears trickling from the corners of her eyes. "I know Buck can handle anything that comes his way, but I still can't stop worrying."

"I know how you feel. Every time Mr. Woodby steps outside, I worry until he's back in the house. He can be cantankerous and stubborn, but I love that man." She smoothed a hand over Angela's hair. "You love Buck, don't you?"

Angela sniffed, her heart squeezing hard in her chest. She'd always loved Buck. From the day she'd met him in medical school, she'd known he was the man for her. Even when he'd broken her heart, she'd never stopped loving him. Why, oh, why had she told him she only wanted to be friends? She loved the man with all of her heart and didn't want to live another day without him in her life.

She prayed she'd have the opportunity to tell him. In the meantime, she needed to be strong and ready to go whenever he returned.

Angela straightened and rubbed her hand over her face, drying her tears. "Thank you for letting me blubber like a baby."

"Angela, we're human. We're allowed to cry on occasion. There's no shame in emotion. Especially when we're stressed about the ones we love." She patted Angela's hand. "Now, come. Let's have that tea. It always calms me to fix a cup and sip while I'm waiting."

Angela let Mrs. Woodby lead her into the kitchen when she'd rather have stood by the window and counted the minutes Buck was away.

"How long have you and Mr. Woodby been together?"

The older woman set the teakettle on a camp stove and lit the burner. "We've been together since we were in grade school. Oh, there was a time we weren't dating, just after we graduated high school. Mr. Woodby didn't want me to wait for him while he went away to seminary. He wanted me to date other men to know for certain what I wanted in a husband."

Her smile softened and her eyes grew cloudy with memories as she stared at the heating kettle.

"And did you?" Angela asked. "Did you date other men?"

Mrs. Woodby grinned. "I did. And you know what I learned?"

"What?" Angela leaned toward the woman, eager to hear more.

"That Mr. Woodby was the only man for me. He was like the other half that made me whole. Without him, my life wasn't full." The kettle heated until the steam made a whistling sound. The minister's wife filled a cup with hot water from the kettle and dropped a tea bag into it. She handed the cup to Angela and motioned for her to take a chair at a small table. She filled another cup and sat across from Angela, dipping her tea bag in the hot water. "You know what I mean, don't you? You and Buck are so in love, you must feel the same way. I see it in your eyes."

Angela's chest filled with all the love she felt for Buck, and her cheeks heated. She pressed her palms to her face. Did it show that much? Could Buck see through her when she'd said she wanted to be "just friends"? Did he know she'd been lying?

Hell, she wanted all those things she'd wanted back in medical school and more. She wanted the happily-ever-after life with the man she loved. If it meant risking her heart again for a chance to be with him, so be it. If he left her again, well, she'd already proven to herself she could survive. It would be hard, but any time with Buck was better than never seeing him again. Why hold back when she could have him now?

She lifted the cup of tea to her lips and sipped. Despite Mrs. Woodby's promise that drinking a cup of tea would calm her, she found herself wanting to leap to her feet and rush to the window. Sitting still was killing her.

Finally, she set her cup on the table and stood. "I don't know how you remain so calm. I'm not nearly as patient. I have to move."

"By all means. Each person handles stress in his or her own way." Mrs. Woodby remained at the table sipping her tea.

Angela strode to the window, anxious to catch sight of Buck and Mr. Woodby returning on the motorcycle. As she leaned toward the gap between the boards over the window, she was shocked to see more of Koku's men in front of the house, at the door. They were different men than those who'd come earlier, but dressed the same and brandishing rifles.

"We have trouble," Angela said softly enough not to be heard through the door. She turned to Mrs.

Woodby, the blood rushing from her face. "Get to the basement."

Someone banged on the door and shouted for them to open the door. Mrs. Woodby set down her cup and stood, her eyes rounded. She rose from her seat at the table and went to the hidden doorway. She raised her hand but didn't get the chance to press it to the wall before the door slammed inward, the brace board over it splitting into two pieces.

Angela squealed and backed away from the men storming through the entrance.

She hadn't gotten far when one of them grabbed her arm and dragged her across the floor.

Mrs. Woodby yelled, "Leave her alone!" She grabbed a pillow from the floor and went after the man dragging Angela toward the door. She hit the man with the pillow, but its softness did little to deter the man from taking Angela.

Angela fought hard, but the man who'd grabbed her was much bigger and stronger than she was.

Mrs. Woodby hit the man again with the pillow, reminding Angela of a teenage pillow fight party. The attack with the pillow would do little to save her from being taken. But she had to give the old woman credit for having the gumption to help her.

Another man grabbed the minister's wife around

the middle, lifted her off the ground and set her away from the man dragging Angela toward the exit.

The older woman made one last effort to get the man to let go of Angela, but he wasn't taking suggestions from anyone, much less an old woman with a soft, cushy pillow.

Mrs. Woodby kept swinging, but nothing was stopping the men from taking whatever they wanted. And apparently, they wanted Angela.

She kicked, bit, scratched and fought her hardest, but the men were stronger and there were more of them than she could fight off.

The minister's wife fought valiantly for her, but she and her pillow were no match for the men.

One man grew tired of her assaults and backhanded her, sending her flying across the room.

She slammed against a wall and slid to the floor, unconscious.

"Leave her alone!" Angela cried and struggled even harder to free herself to go to the old woman. She could be dead or dying for all she knew. As a doctor, she might be able to help. But only if the men holding her would let her go long enough to render aid.

They didn't relinquish their holds on her arms.

The largest man bent low, grabbed her legs and flung her over his shoulder.

With her legs trapped under his arm, all she could do was beat against the man's back with her fists. It was as if she were tickling him. He laughed and strode through the door and out into the late afternoon sunshine.

Sweet heaven, where was Buck?

All she could think as they dragged her away was *Please, Buck, help me!*

Chapter Eleven

Buck didn't have time to reach for the gun beneath his jacket. Instead, he hid his hip and hand behind the motorcycle and reached for the Ka-Bar knife strapped to his side in time to jerk it from its scabbard and jab the wickedly sharp blade into the gut of the first man to reach him.

His attacker screamed and fell to the ground, clutching at his abdomen.

When the others saw what had happened to their compadre, they launched themselves at Buck.

He dived over the top of the motorcycle, hit the ground and rolled to his feet. If he didn't strike fast, the attackers would pull their weapons and start shooting. Seven against one wouldn't last long. He'd be bullet-ridden and useless.

His only hope was to go on the offensive. Strike first and fast. Holding the knife in front of him, Buck leaped at the first man, sliced him across his throat, spun him around to catch the blade of another man and shoved him away. Moving fast, he vaulted back over the bike and planted both feet into another man's chest as that guy raised his rifle. He knocked him into the man behind him.

Both men went down, their rifles flying from their hands.

Buck snatched one of the weapons, fired and killed the two men on the ground. He dropped behind the bike and came up swinging the butt of the weapon at the head of one of the other men.

Shots rang out, one of the bullets hitting Buck. The projectile sliced through the edge of his arm, leaving a shallow, bloody trail.

Buck barely felt the pain, adrenaline pumping through his veins, making his heart pound and his pulse race. He turned the rifle on the other two men fumbling to aim their weapons and pulled the trigger, hitting them with several rounds each in the chest. Then he dived for the side of a building, out of range of other would-be assassins. From his position, he took down the rest, easy targets for a seasoned navy SEAL.

When the gunpowder smoke cleared, Buck tallied his results. Seven of Koku's men lay on the ground. But there had been more than these men in the trucks that had passed through town earlier. Had they made it back to the Woodbys' house?

Buck checked in all directions before running to the motorcycle. The first thing he noticed was the acrid scent of gasoline. The bright stain in the dirt made his gut clench. One of the stray bullets had pierced the tank. He didn't have time to waste if he planned to get back to the Woodby house on what was left of the gas in the tank.

Mr. Woodby eased out of the building, his eyes wide, his hand pressed to his chest. "I consider myself a forgiving man, but these men had long ago gone past forgiveness."

Buck didn't have time to philosophize over the dead. He had to get back to Angela, ASAP. Instinct told him something wasn't right. He felt it deep down, and the distance between him and the woman he loved was far too great.

"Going back to the house?" Mr. Woodby asked.

"I am." He slung his leg over the seat. He only had moments to get to the house before all of the gasoline leaked out of the tank. "If you're coming, get on."

The minister swung his leg over the seat and held on around Buck's belly.

Praying he didn't start a fire with the leaking gas, Buck cranked the engine and twisted the throttle, taking his chances, hoping against hope he didn't set them both aflame. He was willing to take any risk to get to Angela as quickly as possible.

He spun the bike around and headed down the back streets they'd come in on. Through the lanes and alleyways, Buck kept watch for other vehicles running the parallel main road a couple blocks away. At one point, a truck lumbered by with a contingent of Koku's men wielding rifles and shouting.

Buck was happy to avoid that bunch of thieves, thugs and terrorists. He'd had enough struggles for the day, and his body still hurt from fighting Koku's men.

When he reached the white stucco building that was the Woodbys' home, he could feel the silence stretch before him like a cloak of sadness.

He waited impatiently while Woodby slipped off the back, and then he jumped up and ran for the front door. "Angela!"

She didn't respond.

The branches on the tree beside the house waved gently in the breeze, unconcerned with the plights of men.

Even before he reached the door, he could see it stood slightly open. The doorjamb was splintered and the bar that should have been securely wedged over the door had been snapped into two pieces.

Buck ran into the building, searching for the love of his life. "Angela!"

A moan sounded from the corner of the small living space.

Mrs. Woodby lay on her side against the wall, her eyes blinking open. She touched a hand to the back of her head and winced. "W-what happened?"

"Gladys?" The minister rushed in after Buck and ran to his wife. He dropped to his knees beside her and gathered her gingerly into his arms. "Oh, my love. What have they done to you?"

Mrs. Woodby moaned. "Oh my God. I remember. Koku's men came back." She leaned into her husband, tears slipping from her eyes. "They took Angela. Oh dear Lord, they took Angela."

Buck's heart lodged firmly in his throat, choking off his air. He ran through the small house, looking for her, knowing what Mrs. Woodby said was the truth. Angela was gone. Captured by the group of terrorists he'd come to destroy.

He no longer had the time or the means to find the coordinates for Koku's camp. The warlord had to be close, though, if they were terrifying this town on a regular basis.

Buck headed for the door, his mind made up, the only course of action clear.

"Where are you going?" Mr. Woodby called out after him.

"To get help," Buck responded.

He climbed onto the motorcycle and sent a silent prayer to the heavens that the bike would make it back to where he'd stashed his gear bag and the satellite phone. He was glad he'd left it outside of town. If he'd had it on the bike, the bullets that had pierced the gas tank might also have taken out his only means of communicating with his team.

The smell of gasoline was strong, but he couldn't let that worry him. The motorcycle had to get him back to his bag. Buck held his breath and started the engine. It puttered and then engaged. Without waiting to see if it would remain running, he shifted into gear and twisted the throttle.

The bike leaped onto the road headed north out of town. He didn't care if someone followed him. If anyone got in the way of him calling for help, he'd shoot first and ask questions later. Angela had been captured by a ruthless murderer. His only focus was getting to her before the warlord hurt her.

No one tried to stop him. No one stepped into his path, and the road was clear of all traffic. A mile from town, the bike sputtered, coughed and died. All the gas he'd put into the tank had leaked out, leaving the motorcycle to function as one large paperweight.

Buck left the bike and took off on foot, running as fast as his legs would take him to the last place he and Angela had made love.

By the time he returned to the copse of trees, he was ready to run the gauntlet of the lion pride. Thankfully, the field in front of the stand of brush and trees was empty.

Buck didn't take it for granted. The pride could very easily have taken up residence in the clearing beyond the line of brush. He slowed and eased his way through the thick branches, his gun in hand, his senses heightened, his guard up in case he came face-to-face with one of the savannah's most deadly predators.

For once, fate played into his hands. The tiny clearing was empty and the gear bag was where he'd left it in the branches. He pulled out the phone, hit the buttons that would connect him with his team and waited for them to answer.

"Buck, where the hell have you been?"

The relief he felt at the sound of Big Jake's voice sent Buck to his knees. "They have her. Koku's men captured Angela."

"Damn," Big Jake said. "I hate to hear that. She's a good woman with a big heart. But…the good news is that we're on our way from Djibouti. The commander got tired of waiting for you and sent us out to bring you in."

"I'm not going back until we get Angela out of Koku's clutches."

"Understood. And you're in luck. We're fully loaded for bear and ready for a fight."

Buck let go of the breath he felt like he'd been holding since he'd left the Woodbys' house. "ETA?"

"Within the hour," Big Jake responded. "Stay where you are. We have the satellite phone on our GPS tracking device. We'll find you, and the team will take it from there."

Buck had never been more appreciative of the brotherhood that was the navy SEALs than he was at that moment. They had his back and they wouldn't let him down.

He prayed he wasn't too late to save Angela.

THE MEN WHO'D taken Angela had tied her wrists and ankles, dragged a burlap sack over her head, and thrown her into the back of a truck. They'd bumped along a rough road for what felt like a very long time but was probably less than an hour.

Every inch of her body felt bruised by the rough ride, but Angela couldn't worry about the aches and pains. She had to worry instead about being killed. Throughout the ride, she'd worked at the bindings, trying to get her hands free, but the ropes were too tight. All she managed to accomplish was to rub her wrists raw in the process.

Her ankles were a different story. She wiggled and twisted until she was able to work the rope free. Whoever had tied them hadn't secured the binding tight enough, which worked to her advantage. She had her feet free, even if she couldn't move her hands from behind her back. All of her wiggling and twisting had the added benefit of shifting the burlap over her head. She could see light if she moved just right.

When the truck stopped bumping and the engine shut off, Angela knew she had to make a break for it, or suffer at the hands of Koku. He'd been known to rape and kill women without showing a shred of compassion.

If she could get to the edge of the camp, she might have a chance of escaping. Then she could think about how to evade the wild animals who preyed on defenseless creatures. She'd much rather face a pride of lions than Koku and his men.

Though she was scared and worried about her fate, Angela wasn't ready to give up. She would get free and go back to Buck, or die trying. Hopefully, the dying part wouldn't be the endgame. She had things she wanted to tell Buck, and she refused to die until she had the chance to let him know just how much she loved him and always had.

Men moved around her, jumping out of the truck and onto the ground.

Someone grabbed her ankles and yanked her toward the edge of the truck bed. The burlap bag caught on something and was dragged off her head, allowing her to see without obstruction and to study her surroundings before she was unceremoniously flung over a man's shoulder and carried toward a building.

She couldn't use her hands to steady the bouncing and she flopped like a rag doll, a bony shoulder jabbing into her gut. Her head smacked into the man's back as they crossed the rough ground.

They came to a building at the center of the camp, the only one with four sturdy walls and a roof. It had likely been a farmer's home until Koku had commandeered it for his operations center. All around her were pens that might once have held goats and cattle, but were now topped with concertina wire. Inside were the young men and boys who'd been taken from their families and forced into service for Koku's army.

In one area, young teenage boys were being drilled in how to march and display the proper respect for their superiors. They weren't caged like animals, having already been indoctrinated and brainwashed into loyalty toward Koku and his cause.

The man carrying her stopped in front of the building and knocked on the wooden door.

Angela couldn't see what was going on from her position staring at the man's backside.

He exchanged words with the man who opened the door. Moments later, he entered the building and walked down a shadowy hall to a room with more light.

Once inside the room, he dumped her on the floor and backed through the doorway, leaving Angela to figure out how to sit up when her arms were secured behind her back. She drew her knees beneath her and pushed to a kneeling position to face the man behind a metal desk. Two massive men stood on either side of him, each holding a rifle, their faces masks of determination.

"You are Angela Vega, the doctor who left the refugee camp in Bentiu a couple days ago." The man behind the desk didn't ask. His words were a statement, a fact.

She stiffened. How did he know who she was?

He smiled, his teeth the whitest part of his dark and dangerous face. "I sent my men to get a doctor, and they came back without one." He drummed his long fingers on the desk. "You have been a difficult person to track down."

She managed to stand, lifting her chin high. "Maybe I don't want to be tracked."

He waved his hand to the side, dismissing her words. "You have no choice. We need a doctor. You will be our doctor."

"You can't hold me forever," she said.

"And who will stop Koku?" He pounded a fist to his chest and sneered. "No one dares to stop the great Koku. They fear him."

"Do you always refer to yourself in third person?" Angela asked, though she was careful to remove all sarcasm from her tone. The man didn't appear to have a sense of humor. Angela didn't relish the idea of him being angered at her lack of respect for his inflated ego.

Koku's eyes narrowed. "What is this third person you speak of?"

"Nothing." Angela glanced around the room. "Why do you need a doctor?"

"We have sick children and injured soldiers," he said.

"Are you referring to the children you stole from their homes?"

A frown drew his eyebrows together at the center of his forehead. "I bring children here to give them a better life than if they stayed with their poor families. Here they will be fed, have purpose, learn self-discipline and become soldiers."

"Soldiers you will use to terrorize farmers, women and more children." Angela glared at the man who'd killed so many and was maniacally proud of the fact.

He studied Angela. "I see that you do not approve of my methods to bring order and calm to the chaos of this region."

"From what I've seen, you are part of the reason there is chaos."

"You know nothing of the struggles that are here in South Sudan."

"I know you steal the food destined for the refugee camps, and you take children from their parents to train for your army."

"You are from the West, where everyone is governed by one set of rules. In the Sudan, whoever is strongest makes the rules." He pounded his chest again. "I am the strongest. I make the rules."

She wasn't going to convince the man otherwise. He'd built himself up in his mind to larger than life and better than anyone else. Who was she, a female from a foreign land, to tell him he was wrong?

All she could hope for was to survive long enough for Buck and his team to find her and rescue her, along with all of the children being held hostage.

She sighed and played along with what Koku wanted. "Why do you need a doctor?"

He stood, holding a hand to his abdomen. "I have need of you to determine what it is causing me great pain in my side. And when you're done with that, we have at least a dozen men and boys who are dying, and we have been unsuccessful in determining the cause."

"I'll need my backpack with my medical equipment and supplies."

"I have everything you will need. We took things from the hospital tent at the refugee camp. I had my men construct a hospital tent specifically for administering to the people of this camp." He rounded the desk, still holding his side. His lips pressed tightly together and his back hunched with every step. The man was in a great amount of pain and was trying to hide it. "You will come with me."

She refused to move. "I will be unable to help anyone with my hands tied behind my back."

Koku barked an order to one of the men standing by his desk.

The man pulled a knife out of a scabbard on his belt and advanced on Angela.

She backed away, fearing he would jam the blade into her ribs.

Koku gave a short laugh. "He will not hurt you,

as long as you do not hurt me. Be certain you do not harm me in any way. My men have orders to kill you if you do. Do you understand?"

Angela nodded. "I'm a doctor. I took an oath to help people, not hurt them."

"Oaths are mere words. I've known many people who do not live by their words."

"I'm not one of them."

The man with the knife circled her, grabbed her wrists and hacked through the ropes.

When her hands were free, she rubbed at the raw wounds where the ropes had ravaged her skin.

Koku stepped past her, walking slowly out of the building.

His two guards closed in around Angela. When one reached out to grab one of her arms, she glared at him. "You don't have to drag me. I'll go on my own two feet."

The two narrowed their eyes and blocked her from going any other direction than the way their boss was headed.

Angela followed Koku out of the building and toward a crisp white tent perched on flat ground on the other side of one of the pens.

A man met them at the door of the tent and flung open the flap, holding it to the side as Koku and Angela entered.

She thought for a moment she recognized him. Her gaze dropped to where his pant leg was torn and stained with dried blood.

Kaleel.

He didn't meet her gaze; instead he pretended he didn't see her at all.

Of course, he wouldn't want Koku to know she had been the one to stitch his leg. If Koku knew, he'd ask him why he hadn't told him sooner where to find the doctor he'd been searching for.

Angela realized she had information she could hold over Kaleel if he decided to make her life miserable. She tucked that little bit of knowledge away and studied the hospital tent.

It appeared to be like the one the Doctors Without Borders had provided for her to use. Most likely, it had been on one of the shipments destined for another refugee camp.

Angela bit down on her lip to keep from saying something about the theft. Stealing from others didn't seem to concern Koku. He appeared to think it was his right and part of his role as reigning warlord of the region.

Not only had they stolen the tent, they'd stolen the cots and adjustable examination table. All they needed now was the generator, lights and medical equipment and they'd have a fully equipped hospital.

Koku said something to one of the men standing nearby. The man flipped a switch, and the roar of a generator filled the silence. Lights blinked on overhead, chasing out the shadows of the afternoon sunshine that couldn't quite make it through the fabric of the tent.

Angela's eyebrows rose in challenge. "Medical equipment?"

Koku waved toward a shiny white cabinet. "You will find a large collection in there."

She opened the cabinet and found enough tools and supplies to operate a field hospital for several days in a mass casualty event.

Koku hopped onto the examination table. "Now, make this quit hurting."

Angela lifted her chin, disliking the way he demanded instead of asking. "And if I don't?"

"You die." He lay back on the table, wincing as he did. "And if I die…you die."

"Sounds like I don't have much choice in the matter."

"You have a choice. You can fix what is hurting me, or I can turn you over to my men for their pleasure before they kill you." He closed his eyes, his lips pressing together into a tight, thin line.

The doctor in Angela couldn't let the man continue to suffer. She lifted his shirt and pressed her fingers on his belly.

He flinched.

After a thorough examination, measuring his vital signs and talking through his symptoms, she knew what was wrong but wasn't happy with her alternatives. "Your appendix is inflamed. You need to have it taken out before it ruptures."

"Then do it," Koku said through gritted teeth.

"I'm not a surgeon. What you need is a real hospital with a surgeon to operate."

He leaned up on his elbow and glared at her. "You will perform the surgery and you will take this appendix out."

"I told you, I'm not a surgeon. I've never performed this surgery on my own."

"But you've done the procedure with another doctor?"

"During my surgical internship. But I'm not a surgeon."

"Is the necessary medical equipment available here?"

She'd gone through the cabinet. It had what a surgeon would need to perform the procedure. "I think so."

Koku lay back on the table. "Then get started."

"You don't understand."

He waved one of his guards over to him, jerked a pistol out of a holster on the man's belt and pointed it at Angela. "What more do I need to say?"

Angela stared down the barrel of the gun. "I'll get started."

Chapter Twelve

Buck paced in the copse of trees for the next hour, counting every second of every minute until he heard the thumping sound of rotor blades whipping the air. He shoved through the branches and brush to emerge into the open. He barely remembered to look for the pride of lions. At that point, he didn't care. *Koku has Angela* played through his brain like a broken record, and the longer he had her, the worse it could be for her.

Three helicopters flew in from the north. One dropped to the ground long enough for Buck to climb on board. As soon as he was strapped in, the chopper rose into the air and headed south along the road through the town where the Woodbys lived and where Angela had been taken.

Buck filled Big Jake in on what had occurred and his suspicion that Koku couldn't be too far from where they were.

Mustafa had said five towns. They'd gone through three. Only two more remained, and then they would find Koku and hopefully recover Angela before the warlord had a chance to harm her.

Mustafa's journey on foot had taken days. On a motorcycle, keeping out of sight and moving by night had taken far longer than Buck had liked. But in a helicopter, it should be only a matter of minutes before they found Koku's camp. If the sun would stay up long enough. Unfortunately, day was quickly turning into night. Shadows lengthened and blended into the murky gray of dusk.

Before the light was completely snuffed out, Buck counted two more small villages, just like Mustafa had mentioned. Which meant they were getting close to Koku's camp.

Buck leaned over the backs of the pilot and co-pilot's seats to stare out at the landscape ahead. A light blinked and flickered on the ground. He didn't expect Koku's camp to have electricity. Any light would most likely come from a vehicle's headlights, a campfire or battery-operated lanterns. Unless the man commandeered generators to run electricity.

Again, he saw the flicker of lights.

"Did you see that?" He pointed toward the light. The pilot nodded.

"Don't get any closer," Big Jake said. "If that's

the camp, we need the element of surprise in order to take on a much larger force."

Adrenaline flowed through Buck's system, firing his blood and making him anxious to hit the ground and get to the business of rescuing Angela. But he knew Koku had a lot of dangerous men working for him. They needed to recon the area, find out what they were up against before they could plan the mission.

All of which took time. And time might not be in Angela's favor.

Two helicopters landed an estimated two miles from what they guessed was the target. The third chopper, containing Buck, Big Jake, Pitbull, Harm, T-Mac and Diesel, continued in a wide circle, far enough out not to alert the occupants of the camp with their engine and rotor noise. They flew close to the earth, to keep from being spotted, with exterior lights off.

Several times they saw lights blink on then off. By this time, they'd determined the lights were headlights from the trucks Koku used to transport his men.

"That has to be it," Buck said. "Angela is down there."

"We'll get her out," Big Jake assured him. "But we can't go in there like John Wayne, guns a-blazin'.

We need a plan, and we need to know how many of Koku's men we'll be up against."

Buck understood what Big Jake was saying, but his heart was telling him to *go, go, go!*

He'd left Angela once and it had nearly killed him. Leaving her this time had left her exposed to Koku's men. Buck had let her down. By trying to keep her out of the line of fire, he'd left her in a vulnerable situation she had no way of escaping.

Their pilot flew back to the location where the other two helicopters had landed. The men disembarked and checked their weapons and communications. In all, there were eighteen SEALs ready to do whatever it took to take out Koku and rescue the American doctor. The helicopters would be on standby to extract them when they needed them to come. Until then, they would stay back, out of range of rocket-propelled grenades and gunfire.

The two miles into the camp wouldn't take the SEALs long to cover. They were all in top physical condition and knew the stakes. What would take time was easing up to the camp, locating any guards on the perimeter and neutralizing the chance of them alerting the rest of the camp to the infiltration.

The team had been on enough missions together to know what it took.

Buck took point, leading the team into Koku's

territory. As soon as they got close, they split off, establishing their own circle to identify guard posts.

"Got one Tango on the northeast boundary," Pitbull reported. "He appears to be asleep."

"Tango on eastern edge," Harm whispered.

Buck spotted movement in the shadow of a tree. He lowered his night-vision goggles over his eyes and picked up the green heat signature of a warm body. "I've got one on the north."

"You know what to do," Big Jake said.

"Affirmative," Buck, Pitbull and Harm responded.

They would move in, quietly dispatch the guards and cover while the other bounded forward.

Buck sneaked up on his guard. The man was equipped with an AK-47 rifle, an old one probably supplied by the Russians. He didn't even have time to shout or react, and Buck was on him. Seconds later, the threat was eliminated.

"North Tango down," Buck said into his radio.

"East Tango down," Harm's voice said into his ear.

Moments later, Pitbull came over the radio. "Northeast Tango down."

"Let's do this," Big Jake said. "Cover."

"Got your six," Buck replied.

While the six of them moved forward, the others

circled the camp and eliminated guard positions one by one, reporting in as they accomplished the tasks.

Buck's team moved forward, edging closer to the camp where they could get an accurate count of what they were up against.

Men moved around a fire pit, where a large spit had been erected and the carcass of some kind of deer was slowly being roasted. The smell of succulent flesh met Buck's nostrils, reminding him that he hadn't eaten a decent meal in days. His stomach growled, but he ignored it, knowing Angela was somewhere in that camp, possibly in pain, maybe tortured or raped.

His gut clenched at the thought, and it was all he could do to keep from rushing in to find her.

"I count fifty-four," Diesel said.

"I got fifty-five," Big Jake said. "There might be some lying on the ground in the shadow of that building."

"There's an entire corral full of children close to where I am," Harm reported.

"Any sign of Angela?"

"No. But there's a large tent in the center of the camp. She could be in there or in the building."

"I'll take the tent," Buck said.

"Harm, you're with Buck," Big Jake said. "Pitbull, you're with me. Diesel and T-Mac will provide cover.

Give us ten minutes to locate the doctor. If we're not back by then, make some noise."

"Give me a minute to set up the noise factor diversion," T-Mac said.

"Do it," Big Jake said. "And report back."

A few moments later, T-Mac came across the radio. "Diversion fireworks are in place."

Buck touched the grenades he had strapped to his protective vest, gripped his rifle, settled his night-vision goggles in place and prepared to enter Koku's camp.

ANGELA HAD SWEAT her way through an operation she'd only assisted with on five occasions during her internship that seemed like a million years ago.

Koku insisted on being awake throughout the procedure. She could only give him local anesthesia to deaden the area where she'd be cutting through his skin. Thankfully, the medical kit that had come with the tent and equipment had an instruction book detailing some of the more common operations that could be performed in a field environment. The short review she conducted prior to setting the scalpel to Koku's belly was enough to help her remember what it all looked like, and what things to look for once she got inside.

Kaleel served as her nurse, helping to dab at the

blood and hold things when she needed help. He was useless at handing her the different instruments because he didn't know their names.

Angela made it through the operation, removed the diseased appendix and sewed Koku up. When she was done, she washed her hands with alcohol, cleaned the instruments and put them back in the cabinet.

Koku lay on the table, awake, but not as forceful as he'd been before they'd started. He lifted his head just enough to look her way in the overhead light. "You'll take care of the others in the morning," he said and gave a sharp command to his guards, who'd stood back from the operating table the entire time she'd worked on their boss.

The men grabbed her arms and led her from the tent to another, smaller hut with a real door and a lock hasp on the outside.

This was where he'd keep her locked up. If she didn't make her break for it now, she'd never get away. But they had a firm grip on her arms.

Angela pretended to faint, going limp and slipping toward the ground, hoping they'd be surprised and lose their grips on her.

When they did, she rolled sideways, dived between them and made a run for it.

She hadn't gone three steps before they caught

her. One snagged her hair and yanked her backward so hard it brought tears to her eyes.

The other tossed her over his shoulder, flung open the hut's door and dumped her on the dirt floor.

She scrambled toward the door, hoping to duck out before they could slam it shut, but she was too late.

The door almost caught her in the face. She fell backward to avoid being hit and landed on her butt.

She could hear the sound of someone slipping a lock through the hasp and clicking it closed.

Not a single glimmer of light made its way into the hut. She didn't know what else was inside with her, and was almost afraid to find out. But she couldn't stand by and do nothing. She had to find a way out before morning. Koku had made it through the operation, but he could still get an infection and die. And as he'd said, if he died, she died.

Angela pushed to her feet and felt her way around the room. The hut was made of what felt like mud bricks and sticks. The roof was thickly woven thatch, and the whole room was musty and filled with mildew. She pushed at the thatch, but it barely budged. If she had something to cut with, she might hack through the thatch and climb out that way. Making her way around the room again, she felt lower, hoping to find an old wooden box she could break up and splinter, forming a kind of wooden knife. But there were no boxes, no pieces of metal, nothing but a pile of straw and the sound of scurrying feet.

She shivered in the darkness, afraid to sit or lie on the ground. Whatever was scurrying might decide she'd make a good meal to nibble on. Rats and mice carried all kinds of disease, and sometimes plague. No, she'd have to sleep standing up. Hopefully Buck would find her before too long. She'd give anything to lie in his arms and have him chase away all the bad guys and bad things that could happen to her.

She felt her way around to the door again, needing that little bit of spatial grounding to keep her from feeling disoriented and dizzy.

Dear Lord, she'd performed an unassisted operation on a man. She'd cleaned wounds, delivered babies, sewn cuts and even pulled a few teeth, but never had she removed someone's appendix. Her knees shook, then her hands and her entire body trembled as the enormity of what she'd done settled over her.

Though she'd been in Africa for over a year. The closest she'd come to surgery was delivering a breech baby. She hadn't had to perform a cesarean section or any other more invasive procedures. Koku could have died if his appendix had ruptured. He might still die of infection. She'd given him antibiotics just in case, but in a less than sterile environment, anything could happen.

Angela eventually squatted on the floor with her back leaning against the door. She wrapped her arms around her legs and rested her chin on her knees. She struggled to stay awake, but the dark made her feel as though her eyes were already closed, and the drama of the day had taken its toll. She yawned, closed her dry eyes and tried not to think about rodents and men with guns.

Buck would be there soon. She had to believe it. She had to.

A SOUND AT the door made her jerk awake. Angela had no idea how long she'd been asleep. A minute, an hour. She couldn't tell. The hut was just as dark as it had been—so dark she wondered if maybe she was still asleep and she'd dreamed the sound.

Then she heard it again. It sounded like metal on metal. Perhaps the scrape of a key in a lock?

She staggered to her feet and stepped to the side of the door. If someone opened it, she could potentially hide out of sight until he entered, looking for her. Then she could attack him, kick him where it hurt most, hit him over the head as he doubled up and make a run for the woods.

Angela held her breath, waiting for the moment the door opened.

The sound of a metal latch being lifted off the hasp indicated the lock had been removed and the door could be opened.

Ready to spring, Angela waited as the door swung outward.

A light shined into the hut from a flashlight. Then a man stepped through the door, his pant leg tattered and torn.

Kaleel.

He turned the beam to catch his face. He lifted his finger to his lips and jerked his head to the side, indicating she should follow.

What was he doing? Had Koku requested her presence? Should she take this opportunity to make a run for it? Why was Kaleel being so secretive?

He stepped back, looked both directions and waved for her to come with him. Without trying to grab her as the guards had done, he allowed her to move on her own.

Angela stepped through the door, her gaze darting right and left. The camp had gotten quiet. Men were still awake, gathered around a fire pit where some kind of large animal was roasting on a spit. They had torn off strips of meat and were eating eagerly.

Angela's belly rumbled, but she didn't dare follow her hunger.

Kaleel moved into the shadow of the hut and circled around behind it. He pointed toward a stand of trees a hundred yards away from the camp's edge. "You must go, now."

She faced him, looking for weapons. Was he turning her loose so he could shoot her in the back? Or was he doing the decent thing and letting her go?

"Why?" she asked.

"You saved my leg. You are a good doctor." He nodded toward the woods. "Go."

Angela's heart contracted.

The man had risked his life to save her. If Koku found out Kaleel had released her, he'd kill him.

"Come with me," she urged. "Koku will kill you if he knows you released me."

"He will not know," Kaleel assured her. "I will place the lock on the door as if it was never unlocked."

"But someone is bound to have seen you." Angela couldn't let this man take the fall for her.

"The longer you wait, the more dangerous it becomes. Please, go, before he discovers you are gone."

"Too late," a voice said. "I already know."

Kaleel spun to face the man who'd spoken.

Angela froze, her heart stopping for a second and then racing ahead so fast it made her dizzy.

Standing on the other side of Kaleel were Koku and his two guards. He was leaning heavily on one of the men, holding a handgun in his free hand.

"I do not tolerate betrayal among my soldiers," he said.

Angela stepped forward. "Koku, don't sh—"

The warlord pulled the trigger. The shot rang out, extra loud in the quiet of the night.

Kaleel's eyes rounded. He raised a hand to his chest and crumpled to the ground.

Angela screamed and dived for Kaleel.

Koku's other guard caught her before she could reach the man on the ground. He wrapped his thick arm around her body, trapping both of her arms under one of his.

Angela kicked and fought. "Let me help him. Please." Tears streamed from her eyes as she struggled to free herself from Koku's guard.

"He's dead. And you will be, too, if you don't cooperate."

"He was only trying to help me," Angela whispered.

"That man betrayed me. He didn't deserve to live." He nodded to his guard.

The guard dragged her toward the hut again and flung open the door.

Koku followed, held up by his other guard.

The doctor in Angela wanted to tell Koku that he should be resting to allow his incision time to heal, but she couldn't.

Never had she felt such a rush of white-hot hatred for a man. And she'd saved his life. What kind of monster did that make her? She should have taken the opportunity to kill the man while she had the chance. All the children he'd kidnapped, all the men and women he'd tortured and killed. All those he would subject to his brand of terrorism still to come.

Angela hoped his stomach was full of infection and that he'd rot in hell.

Her chance to escape had passed. Not only had she blown her chance to be free, but she'd cost Kaleel his life by delaying her departure. If she hadn't hesitated, he might have gotten away with his plan.

Her heart heavy, Angela could do little against the superior strength of Koku's guard. Even if she could shake free of his grip, Koku would shoot her like he'd shot his own man, Kaleel.

The only hope she had left was that Buck would find her and free her from Koku's madness, without getting shot himself.

Chapter Thirteen

Buck had been heading for the tent when he saw a man being half led, half carried by two other, more burly men. He appeared to be injured, if the bandages around his belly were any indication. And the bandages meant someone had worked on him. Someone who might be a doctor.

His pulse quickened, and his hand tightened on the rifle he carried.

Angela had to be there. Since the man had just exited the tent, she had to be inside the structure, working on someone else or cleaning up.

His focus on the tent and getting there without being spotted, he barely noticed when the three men disappeared around the side of a thatch-roofed hut.

A gunshot rang out, diverting his attention from the tent back to the hut where the three men had gone. One shot fired. What did that mean?

Buck had been halfway across the clearing leading to the camp when the shot echoed in the night air.

"Things are about to get sticky in Camp Koku," Big Jake said. "Lie low until we figure out who fired that round."

Buck dropped in his position and studied the scene.

The men who'd been gathered around the fire had scattered, grabbing their rifles and rushing toward the sound of the gunfire.

"Holy hell, I think we found the doc," Pitbull said.

Buck raised his night-vision goggles and scanned the camp. A pen-like area held dozens of small heat signatures. He'd bet they were the children, corralled like cattle. He swung his head in time to see the three men reappear with another, smaller person in tow. Buck raised his goggles and narrowed his eyes, his heart pounding against his ribs.

Angela.

Buck was halfway to his feet before he realized what he was doing. If one of the men with guns looked his direction, he'd appear as a silhouette. A potential enemy threat. Koku's men didn't strike him as the type to think first, then fire. More likely, they'd shoot first and sift through the bodies later. Buck would be of no use to Angela if someone shot him.

Dropping to the prone position, he watched what was happening.

Men gathered around the two big guys, the injured one and Angela.

The man with the bandages spoke sharply to the gathering of men. They quickly dispersed, returning to the fire, where they laid down their weapons and went back to eating the roasted meat.

The guy holding Angela flung open the door to the hut and tried to throw her inside.

Angela braced her feet on the door frame and refused to go into the hut.

If the situation wasn't so dire, Buck would have chuckled at her bold determination.

That's when he noticed the man with the bandages held a gun in his hand, and he pointed it at Angela.

"We could use that diversion about now. Angela's in trouble. I'm taking the shot," he said into his microphone. He lay against the ground, sighted in on the man holding the gun and squeezed the trigger.

Just as his finger tightened on the trigger, the man holding the bandaged guy shifted, placing his body in between the guy holding the gun and Buck's bullet. The person who'd been holding up the bandaged dude jerked, let go of his charge and toppled to the ground like a felled tree.

"Damn," Buck muttered. He sighted in again, but

he'd missed his opportunity to take down the man holding the gun pointed at Angela.

Before Buck could get his original target in his sights, the man grabbed Angela and held his gun to her temple. He pulled her with him toward the larger building.

Once again, the men surrounding the fire pit grabbed their weapons and raced toward the man and Angela.

The other big guy who'd originally been holding onto Angela used his body as a shield to protect the man now holding a gun to Angela's head.

Buck would bet his best rifle that the man threatening Angela was Koku.

Fiery rage ripped through Buck. He rose from his position and ran toward the camp, keeping low but hardly hiding as he raced toward Koku and Angela.

"Buck, what the heck are you doing? Get down!" Big Jake said. "T-Mac, now would be a good time to let loose that diversion."

Before Big Jake finished giving the command, an explosion lit up the night.

Out of the corner of Buck's eye, he could see T-Mac had made it to one of the trucks in the camp. Moments later, that truck exploded, sending parts flying into the air.

Men yelled and shots were fired as Koku's soldiers panicked and ran in all directions. Soon they were racing for the safety of the trees. Some even abandoned their weapons to keep from slowing down in their flight away from the destruction.

Under the cover of the explosions and resulting flames, Buck ran across the camp, hugging the shadows of the few buildings and tents until he was within a couple yards of Koku and Angela.

Buck dropped beside a pile of boards and tin, assumed a kneeling, supported position, aimed his rifle at Koku, and cursed. He couldn't take the shot for fear of hitting Angela.

Meanwhile the members of his team were closing in on those of Koku's soldiers who'd remained to fight the threat they had yet to identify. To start with, all they knew was that things were exploding around them.

The SEAL team picked them off until the last few threw down their weapons and ran for the woods.

Which left Koku, his bodyguard and Angela.

"I'll shoot her!" Koku shouted.

"The hell you will!" Angela jammed her elbow into the man's bandaged belly, ducked her head away from the handgun and twisted backward out of Koku's grip.

The bodyguard dived for her as a shot rang out. All three of them fell to the ground.

Too far away from Angela to do anything, Buck leaped to his feet and ran, his throat tight, his heart squeezing in his chest.

Had Angela been hit? He couldn't tell. All he could see was the bodyguard, piled on top of Koku and Angela. No one was moving.

As he reached them, Buck could see a hand, holding a gun, rise out of the pile.

He dived to the side as Koku fired. The bullet grazed his shoulder, but he was on his feet before Koku could aim and fire again.

Koku turned the gun toward Angela, who lay trapped beneath the big bodyguard.

Buck did the only thing he could—he threw himself onto Koku to deflect the bullet from hitting Angela.

The gun went off.

Buck held still, waiting for the pain. When it didn't come, he rolled to the side.

Koku lay still on the ground. Buck kicked the handgun from his grip, sending it flying into the darkness.

He couldn't see Angela's eyes, and he couldn't tell if she was moving. He slung his rifle over his shoulder, grabbed hold of the bodyguard and dragged his dead weight off Koku and Angela.

If Koku so much as blinked, he'd shoot the bastard.

Finally, he was able to lift Angela into his arms. "Angela? Sweetheart, tell me you're okay. Please."

She smiled up at him. "I think I passed out. I couldn't breathe with that man lying on top of me. And then I thought Koku shot you. Then everything went blank."

"You weren't hit, were you?" He silently cursed the darkness, wishing he could shine a searchlight over her body to make sure she wasn't bleeding.

"No. I'm fine now that I can breathe." She wrapped her arms around his neck and kissed his lips. "I was determined to live. I have so much I want to say to you."

He kissed her back and set her on her feet. "Hold that thought. We need to make sure you and all the kids are safe."

Angela grinned, the white of her teeth the only indication of her expression in the darkness. "I feel safer already."

There were still sounds of gunfire and people yelling. Buck couldn't relax until Angela was safely out of Koku's camp.

"Sweetheart, standing around with bullets flying is never a good idea. We should go." He slid his rifle off his shoulder and held it in his right hand, and secured Angela's hand in his left.

ANGELA HELD ON to Buck, ready to go anywhere he wanted her to. As they stepped over Koku's bodyguard, something snagged her ankle, making her trip and fall on top of the dead man.

If not for her hold on Buck's hand, she'd have face-planted in the dirt. A shot exploded in the darkness, so loud and so close it rang in Angela's ears.

Buck released her hand, staggered backward, steadied himself and raised his rifle.

Angela started to rise.

"Stay down!" Buck shouted.

Her heart hammering in her chest, Angela rolled off the bodyguard onto her back on the ground and looked up in time to see Koku sitting up, aiming a small handgun at Buck. He fired the weapon at the same time Buck pulled the trigger on his rifle and sent several rounds into the warlord's chest.

Koku fell back and lay still on the ground.

Angela pushed to her feet, her pulse nowhere close to returning to normal. "Is he dead? Did you kill him?"

Buck didn't answer.

Turning, Angela was just in time to see Buck drop to his knees and keel over, still holding his rifle, but also clutching a hand to his midsection.

"Buck!" Angela dropped to her knees beside him,

forcing back the panic and drawing on every bit of knowledge she'd gained in school and working as a doctor. She ripped open his jacket and shirt, pushing the fabric out of the way with her fingers. "Do you still have that flashlight?"

"Inside pocket of my jacket," Buck said through clenched teeth.

She fumbled through his jacket, located the flashlight and shined it down at the wound. Even with the little bit of light, she couldn't see the damage. She needed more light and an operating room. For the moment, all she could do was stop the bleeding by applying pressure. "I need your help, so stay with me."

"Yes, ma'am," Buck said, his voice weak.

"Put your hand here." She guided him, placing his hand over the wound. "Press down."

He did as she'd told him, but she didn't know how long he'd remain alert.

Angela pulled the knife out of the scabbard on his belt and jabbed it into her shirt. Once she got the tear started, she ripped several inches off the hem, ripped it again and folded one half into a pad, the other half into a strip she could use to secure the pad to his belly.

She replaced his bloodied hand with the pad,

holding it down to apply pressure. "Graham, stay with me."

He lay still, making her wonder if he'd passed out. "I'm not going anywhere," he finally muttered.

"Where's your team? I could use a little help to get you to the operating room."

"Operating room?" He chuckled. "Now I know I'm dreaming. Take my headset."

She touched his face and slid her hands over his head until she found the headset. She removed it and placed it over her ears. "Hello?"

"Who's this?"

"This is Angela. Buck was shot. We need help."

"Where are you?"

She glanced around, only then aware of where they were. To Angela, it seemed like ages ago that Koku's bodyguard had tried to lock her in her cell. "In the shadow of the small hut with the thatched roof."

"I'll be right there. The others are still mopping up what's left of the resistance."

They disconnected, and Angela returned her attention to Buck. "I don't know who was talking, but he said he'd be right here."

"Probably Big Jake." Buck tried to sit up.

"What are you doing?" She pressed her hands on his chest, keeping him down. "You could be bleeding internally. I need you to lie still so that you don't bleed to death."

"Would you miss me?"

"Damn right, I would." She glared at him, though he couldn't see her face in the darkness. "You are not leaving me again, in any way, form or fashion. I'm not letting you."

"You tell him, Doc," a voice said behind her.

Angela almost cried in relief, seeing the dark form of a man decked out in combat gear.

Keeping her voice calm, she stood. "We need to get him to the hospital tent as soon as possible."

Another man's shadowy figure appeared behind Big Jake's. "What's happening? I heard Buck was down."

"Not for long," Buck answered from the ground.

Angela recognized the newcomer by his voice as T-Mac.

"Koku had a hospital tent set up. If we could get Buck there, I can examine his wound in better lighting."

"Let's do this." T-Mac handed her his rifle. "Cover us while we're hauling this guy's sorry ass over to the tent."

Angela fumbled with the rifle. "I don't know how to operate this."

Buck chuckled briefly, the sound cut off in a

moan. "Just point and shoot," he managed before going limp.

The two SEALs still standing each slid their arms beneath Buck's shoulders and legs and lifted him in a fireman's seated carry.

"Lead the way," Big Jake ordered.

Carrying the rifle with her hands on the grip, finger on the trigger, Angela led the men to the hospital tent, visible in the light from the fire pit.

Once inside, she had them deposit Buck on the operating table.

"There's a generator somewhere around here. It powers the lights," she said. "Find it and get it started. I need light."

Big Jake chuckled. "Yes, ma'am."

"T-Mac, can you put pressure on the wound with one hand and hold this flashlight with the other while I get him out of some of these clothes?"

"Yes, ma'am," T-Mac answered. He took over, pressed down on the wound and shined the light over Buck's belly, while Angela cut away his shirt and unbuttoned his pants.

"Had I known how easy it was to get a girl to undress me, I'd have shot myself in the gut a long time ago," T-Mac teased.

Any other time, Angela would have laughed, but

not now. Not when Buck's life potentially hung in the balance.

The generator roared to life, and seconds later, lights filled the small tent.

Angela breathed a small sigh of relief and hurried to the cabinet with all the medical supplies and surgical instruments.

She pulled out everything she could think of that she might need to work on Buck, loaded it onto a tray and carried it to the operating table.

She didn't know how Koku had managed to steal all of the supplies, but at that moment she was glad he had. Now, she only had to draw on her limited surgical experience to do whatever it took to make certain Buck lived.

Her hand shook as she scrubbed the area around the wound with a gauze pad and Betadine solution.

A hand caught her wrist and held it.

Startled, she jerked her hand back.

"Hey, beautiful," Buck said.

"Oh, sweet heaven," she exclaimed. "You scared the bejesus out of me."

"Sorry. I just wanted to let you know I was still around, and whatever you do, I know it will be your best."

Her vision clouded as tears welled in her eyes. "I hope whatever I do is enough."

Big Jake hurried into the operating room. "The helicopters are on the way."

"Anyone else injured?" Buck asked.

"Only a few scrapes and bruises. Koku's men were so confused by the explosions, they didn't have time to react."

Buck nodded. "Good."

"We'll have a medic here in a minute to assist the doctor," Big Jake added.

Buck didn't look to Big Jake as he spoke. His gaze remained on Angela. "I have all the medical assistance I need right here." He raised her hand to his lips and pressed a kiss to her palm. "Don't look so worried, sweetheart. I'm going to be all right."

"God, I hope you're correct in that assumption." She wasn't feeling quite as confident. "I'm not a surgeon."

"No, but you were top of our class in medical school." He smiled. "You've got this."

She nodded. Whatever she found, she'd deal with and stabilize him long enough to get him back to proper medical care. "Thanks," she said. "Now shut up and let me concentrate."

Buck winked, threw up a salute and responded with a sharp, "Yes, ma'am."

The medic arrived and helped establish an IV

of fluids, then assisted by handing her instruments when she asked for them.

Less than an hour later, she'd removed the bullet, ascertained that none of his vital organs had been hit and he was going to be okay. She sewed him up, applied a bandage and kissed him soundly before allowing his friends to load him onto the helicopter that would take him to Camp Lemonnier, where a surgeon would double-check her work and hopefully fix anything she might have missed.

Big Jake oversaw Buck's movement on a stretcher from the field hospital to the helicopter, walking alongside Angela as she held Buck's hand all the way.

Once they loaded Buck into the helicopter, Angela stepped in for a moment. "You know I can't go with you, don't you?"

Buck held tightly to her hand. "You're staying to help the children, aren't you?"

She nodded. "I have to. Now that I know you're going to be okay, they need someone to see to their welfare."

Buck nodded. "I don't like it, but I understand."

She pressed a kiss to his lips. "I'll see you soon. At least I hope I will."

"We'll figure it out. I promise." He gripped her hand, refusing to release it for the moment. "I'm not leaving because I want to. If they'd let me stay, you know I would."

She raised his hand to her cheek. "I know. And you know I'd go with you if others didn't need me more desperately, don't you?"

He nodded. "It's who you are. You have a heart the size of Africa. It's why I love you."

Her pulse thundered. He'd said he loved her.

"I hate to break this up, but we need to get ol' Buck here back to Djibouti," Big Jake said. "Commander's orders."

Angela kissed him once more and climbed down from the helicopter.

Big Jake exited the aircraft as well.

"Aren't you going with him?" she asked.

"Diesel and Harm will escort him all the way and make sure he doesn't pinch any nurses." Big Jake chuckled. "He'll be champing at the bit to get back here, but he needs to rest for a little while before rejoining the ranks. In the meantime, we have a bunch of kids to sort through and return to their parents. Our commander authorized me to leave a contingent of men to supervise the deconstruction of this camp and the placement of these children."

Angela's heart swelled. "Remind me to thank your commander and the US Navy for their contribution to making this a better world for these kids."

Big Jake saluted. "Yes, ma'am."

They stood for a moment in the blast of air, dust and debris kicked up by the helicopters as they lifted off the ground and flew into the graying light of dawn. Angela prayed for their swift return to civilization and proper medical care. When they'd disappeared on the horizon, Angela clapped her hands together. "Let's get to work." She wouldn't have time to dwell on what would happen between her and Buck. The children needed her undivided attention. She'd have time later to sort through her feelings and decide what to do next.

One thing was certain—she wanted to be with Buck. She still needed to have that talk with him and tell him how she felt. Preferably when he was conscious and able to understand the depth of her feelings for him.

She loved him and would take any time she could have with him.

Chapter Fourteen

Buck had to admit he wasn't the best patient. He'd given hell to the nurses who'd been assigned to see to his wound care and medications. He'd been insubordinate to the doctor who outranked him, threatening on more than one occasion to leave the small hospital before he'd been properly discharged.

When the doctor had suggested he be transported to the next level of care in Landstuhl, Germany, he'd had a conniption fit and nearly wrecked the IV stand, vital-signs monitors and everything around his bedside.

The nurses had to call in two men from security forces to hold him down while they sedated Buck.

Yeah, he'd been an ass, but all he wanted was to be released and find his way back to South Sudan, where half of his team was still assisting with the evacuation and placement of over thirty boys who'd been stolen from their families to man Koku's army.

Then there were the boys between the ages of eleven and seventeen who'd been brainwashed who had to be dealt with. They didn't know how to fend for themselves and would have gone rogue without some kind of program put in place to take the weapons and militant attitudes out of their hands and minds.

The US Army Special Forces unit would work with the South Sudanese Army and UNICEF to provide the psychological support to prepare them for return to civilian life and their families. Most of the children wanted to go home and were eager to get an education.

The navy SEALs stayed several days to ensure Koku's men didn't return to retake the camp and children. They would hand off their responsibilities once the Special Forces units were in place to provide security during the demobilization of the child soldiers.

Buck had been receiving periodic reports from T-Mac and Big Jake. Angela had done her part to treat the sick and injured and had helped set up a medical facility to take care of the children while their placement was still being determined.

Buck's belly still hurt, but not enough to keep him down. He'd argued at length with the doctor, insisting he was well enough to return to duty and South Sudan to assist with the ongoing efforts.

"Your team will return soon. If your wound is properly healing by then, we'll talk about your return to duty" was all the doctor could promise.

His commander had been by a couple times to check on his progress and to admonish him for giving the medical staff hell. "You must be feeling better to be such a pain in the ass," he declared.

"Sir, I just want to be with my team," he'd responded.

"Your team? Or the pretty doctor?" His commander hadn't bothered hiding his grin. "You'll stay here until the doctor releases you."

"Sir, at the least, I could recuperate in my quarters. I don't need to take up space that could be used on someone in worse shape than I am."

His commander glanced around at the empty beds. "We're not exactly bursting at the seams."

So Buck took to pacing the length of the ward, dragging his IV cart along until they finally unhooked the IV and gave him permission to wear his gym shorts instead of mooning the nurses.

On the third day in the hospital, Buck was ready to climb the walls. His doctor came in and declared that his wound was healing nicely.

"I'll sign your release if you promise to take it easy for the next two weeks. You can't return to duty until then."

"Well, then, what the hell good is my release?" Buck demanded.

"You can spend it moping in your quarters, or you can join your team at the All Things Wild Resort," a voice said from behind him.

Buck spun, then winced when the movement reminded him of his stitches.

Big Jake stood in the doorway, still wearing his four-day-old uniform, covered in dirt and smelling pretty ripe.

Buck couldn't stop himself from grinning. "Big Jake, you old son of a bitch." He crossed to the man, and gave him a huge bear hug, causing more pain when he again pulled at the stitches on his belly. "When did you get back?"

"Just a few minutes ago. I came straight here, because I knew you'd be champing at the bit for news and probably giving the medical staff fits."

Heat climbed up Buck's neck. "Yeah, well, they wouldn't let me get back to the action."

"The action has been turned over to other people now. I spoke to the CO, and we've been granted a pass for the next week. Like I said when I walked in, you can spend your time recuperating in your quarters, or you can join us back at All Things Wild."

Buck set his friend and teammate to arm's length. "I don't understand."

"Since our rest and relaxation was cut short, our commander is going to allow us to continue our vacation back at the resort. He even arranged for helicopter transport to get us there."

"He did?" Buck shook his head. "And he's letting me go?"

"No, he told us to take you before he court-martials you. So get dressed, pack your bag and let's go. The chopper leaves in fifteen minutes."

"What if I don't want to go?" Buck asked.

"You'd rather recuperate in your quarters?" Big Jake's brows rose. "What happened to the Buck I knew who'd rather climb a mountain than be confined to quarters?"

Buck shrugged. "I might want to go somewhere else."

Big Jake shook his head. "If you're thinking of hopping on a plane to go to South Sudan, don't bother. The good doctor isn't there. She's not working for Doctors Without Borders anymore."

"What?" Buck frowned. "Why? Where is she? What happened down there?"

"All I know is, once they turned over the children

to UNICEF, they brought in an entirely new crew of doctors and nurses. She was relieved of her duties."

"And she didn't leave a forwarding address?"

"I don't know that she has one yet." Big Jake crossed his arms over his chest. "So, what's it to be? Are you staying here and moping, or are you going to recuperate in Kenya at the resort?" He glanced over his shoulder and lowered his voice to a whisper. "If I were you, I'd go. The CO isn't too happy with you right now. He says you're a terrible patient and he's ready to send you back to the States."

Buck's chest tightened. Angela was gone from South Sudan. He didn't know how to contact her in Africa or in the States. How was he going to keep his promise to see her soon? With his commander breathing fire about his behavior, he didn't have much of a choice. He could stay and risk being sent back to the States, or go with his team to the resort and recuperate there. "I'll be ready in fifteen."

"Make that thirteen. We've been yapping that long." Big Jake spun and started for the door. "I'm jumping in the shower during that time."

"Good, you smell like a goat."

"Yeah, you would know," he called over his shoulder. "You could use a shower, too."

His nurse was there when he turned around with

his discharge instructions and a big grin. "Can't say I'm sad to see you go."

His cheeks burned. "Look, I'm sorry I was such a bastard."

"No worries," she said. "We're not always at our best when we're sidelined. Just get well soon and stay out of the hospital." She handed him a T-shirt and flip-flops. "Now go. Your buddy was right—you could use a shower."

Thirteen minutes later, Buck was showered, shaved and dressed in his loosest uniform with the buttons on his pants unbuttoned to keep from rubbing his stitches. He had a gear bag with more clothes, his weapon and a pad of paper and pens. While he was laid up, he planned on writing some letters to Angela. He'd also get online and see if he could find her on social media or look up her address back in the States. There had to be a way to find her. He wouldn't give up until he did. He'd take a month of leave if he needed to and spend it all searching for the only woman he had ever loved.

T-Mac, Diesel, Harm, Big Jake and Pitbull were waiting when he reached the helicopter landing pad. They all shook hands, hugged and joked about his injury and what they wanted to do when they got back to their vacation that had been so rudely interrupted by work.

Buck strapped himself into the shoulder harness and sat back, prepared for a couple hours in the air. His injuries must have taken more out of him than he'd thought, because with the monotonous drone of the rotor blades hitting the air and the roar of the engine, he fell asleep within minutes of liftoff.

T-Mac woke him as they landed on the airstrip near the resort, where they were greeted by Talia Montclair, the owner and operator of the All Things Wild Safari and Resort.

When Buck stepped down from the helicopter, his knees buckled and he would have fallen if Diesel and T-Mac hadn't been there to hook his arms over their shoulders and help him get his feet back under him.

"I don't know what's wrong with me," he muttered. "I feel as weak as a newborn kitten."

"Could be you took a bullet to the belly."

"I've been shot before."

"But not in the gut. It tends to hit you a little harder," Harm said. "Trust me, I've been there, done that. It's not something I care to repeat anytime soon." He smiled as Talia hurried forward. "You're a sight for sore eyes."

The black-haired beauty frowned and hurried forward. "I heard one of you had been injured. That'll teach him to step in front of a bullet." She winked.

"If you two could get him to the golf cart, he won't have to walk all the way."

"I can walk," Buck said. "I was just stiff from the ride." He straightened and pushed away from T-Mac and Diesel. "See? Steady as a rock." He swayed slightly and the other two men took a step toward him. "Seriously, I've got this."

"Whatever, but if you face-plant in the dirt and tear open your stitches," Big Jake said, "you'll be on the first helicopter back to Djibouti."

"I'm not going to face-plant. Hell, I was pacing the hospital back at the base every day I was there. I got at least a couple miles a day of PT."

Big Jake shook his head. "Yeah, yeah. Put your money where your mouth is and get your carcass to the lodge. We have a surprise for you."

Buck stepped out, forcing his stiff legs to work into a rhythm that would take him along the twisting path to the main lodge. "Do I get my same cabin?" he asked.

"Yes, you do. We had a little trouble and the guests who'd been in it left early. You all have the same cabins as before." Talia had sent one of her staff ahead with the golf cart and walked with the men toward the lodge.

When the main building came into sight, Buck had to admit, if only to himself, he was glad he didn't have much farther to go. His legs were shaky, and he would give anything for a seat on a comfy sofa where he could stretch his legs and maybe have a beer.

As he neared the lodge, a large cat detached itself from the bushes and stalked toward him.

Buck ground to a stop and backed up a step, running into T-Mac and Diesel in the process. Then he realized the cat was the leopard that had been raised at the lodge since it was a kitten.

"Mr. Wiggins, you naughty boy." Talia strode up to the animal and scratched him beneath his chin. "What are you doing out of the garden?"

T-Mac clapped a hand on Buck's back. "Don't tell me you forgot about the cat."

"I did. But it's all coming back to me now. I think I'll go straight to my cabin, if it's all the same to you guys. Can the surprise wait until morning?"

"You might be able to wait, but I'm sure Pitbull won't want to."

A woman appeared, coming along the path toward them.

Buck's heart leaped until he realized the tall, lanky woman had sandy-blond hair and was grinning at Pitbull.

"Marly?" Pitbull held open his arms and she ran into them. "I thought you'd be in Nairobi still packing your apartment."

"I got done and shipped my things to the States. When I heard you were coming back to the resort, I hitched a ride with a pilot I knew. And here I am."

Pitbull wrapped his arms around her waist, lifted her off the ground and swung her around. "That's the best surprise yet." He kissed her soundly and set her back on her feet.

Buck watched, his heart sinking lower in his belly to hurt right next to his wound. Pitbull had Marly there to hug and hold. Why had he bothered to come to the resort with his teammates when he could have been just as miserable back in his quarters, where he didn't have to put on a game face?

"Hey, don't look so glum." Talia touched his arm.

"I don't feel much like being around people right now."

"Could you make it through dinner?" Talia asked. "I had the chef prepare steaks for all of you, just the way you like them."

He was tired, but the thought of sitting among his team while they laughed and joked made him even crankier and less likely to enjoy the meal. What he wanted was to see Angela, to hold her in his arms and tell her everything he hadn't told her and needed to say before she disappeared out of his life again. "I don't think I'll make it through dinner. I'll catch you guys at breakfast."

Big Jake, a few steps ahead of Buck, turned to face him, his mouth open to say something, but was cut off by Talia, who raised her hand.

"Suit yourself," Talia said. "I'll have someone bring a tray of food to your cabin."

"That's not necessary," Buck said. "I can wait to eat until breakfast." He didn't want anyone to bother him. His brand of misery was best spent alone.

She smiled. "I insist. The chef spent a great deal of time and effort to make the meal as special as the men he's cooking for. Now, you go to your cabin and relax. The food tray will be along soon."

"Thanks," he responded with as much enthusiasm as a man heading into the dentist's office.

"I'm going with you," Big Jake said. "We can't have you passing out on the path and being mauled by tame leopards."

"I can get there by myself." He really wanted to be by himself; he suspected he was in for a big old wallow in self-pity and loneliness, and he didn't want his buddies to witness his transgression. God, he wanted to see Angela so badly, he ached in every part of his body.

"Not taking no for an answer." Big Jake walked alongside him as he split off the main path to head toward the cabins.

They walked in silence until they were out of hearing range of the others.

"You miss her, don't you?" Big Jake asked quietly.

Buck's chest hurt with a pain that had nothing to do with the wound in his gut. "Yeah. I hate that I don't know where she is and that I can't even call her."

"What would you say to her if you could find her?"

"What does it matter what I'd say? I have no idea how to find her. I'm going to ask Talia if I can use her computer tomorrow and do some searching online. Damn it!" He pounded his fist into his palm. "I have to find her. I walked out of her life once. I'm not going to do it again. I made a promise."

They'd arrived in front of the cabin he'd used the last time they'd been there. Big Jake laid a hand on his shoulder. "Whatever you do, when you see her again, don't waste time. Tell her how you feel."

"I will. But who knows when that'll be?" Buck pushed open the door and stepped through. He turned back to Big Jake. "I learned something this last mission."

"Yeah? What's that?"

"You have to grab for happiness when you can. And hold on like there might not be a tomorrow."

Big Jake nodded. "In our line of work, that's very true. Tomorrow is never guaranteed."

"And the only easy day was yesterday." Buck sighed. "Remind me of that tomorrow. Thanks for talking me into coming."

"Trust me when I say you'll be glad you did." And with that parting comment, Big Jake left Buck to settle in.

Once inside, Buck bypassed the sofa and headed for the bed, where he could stretch out and give his gut a break from being in a sitting position for two hours on a helicopter. He lay down, intending to rest, not sleep, shielding his eyes from the late-afternoon glare shining through the window. He had lots to think about, but suddenly, he couldn't think anymore.

He must have dozed off, because the next thing he knew, someone had opened the door.

"Put the tray on the table. I'll eat when I feel like it," he said without glancing up from beneath his arm still resting over his eyes. Night had settled in around the cabin, eliminating the need to shield his eyes. When he lowered his arm, he could see the silhouette of a woman in the darkness of the cabin. She set the tray on the table and straightened.

Something about the way she held herself, the way her hair lay around her head and the swell of her hips and breasts struck a chord of recognition. His breath lodged in his throat, and his heart stopped beating.

"You should eat to keep up your strength," she whispered.

"Angela?" He blinked and tried to sit up, forgetting he still had stitches across his belly. He swore and rolled to his side.

By the time he could finally sit on the side of the bed, she was there beside him, switching on the lamp by his bedside. And then she touched his shoulder, spreading fire throughout his mind, body and soul.

"Angela," he breathed as if for the first time, like a baby being born into the world. She was there. Whereas before he'd felt his life had ended, it now had begun, with Angela in it.

He wrapped his arms around her waist and pulled her between his knees, resting his cheek against her breasts. "When? How?" He laughed. "Oh, who cares. You're here now. That's all that matters."

She chuckled and lifted his face to stare into his eyes. "You ruined our surprise."

"Not from where I'm standing. Or sitting." He captured her face in his hands and pulled her down to kiss her like it might be the last kiss they would ever share. He wanted each time he kissed her to be like that. Like every kiss could be their last. He had to make it special, make her love him as much as he loved her.

Never had he been more aware of the fact that tomorrow wasn't guaranteed. He had to take full advantage of today. With this woman. The one he loved.

Chapter Fifteen

Angela had counted every minute between the time she'd watched Buck fly off in that helicopter to when she'd seen him lying in bed in the quaint little cabin at the All Things Wild Resort. Though she'd been busy caring for frightened and confused children, administering aid and comforting those who were so homesick they cried and cried, Buck was always on her mind.

And now he was here, holding her.

"I have to tell you something."

"Wait. I want to say something first." He pushed to his feet, swayed a little and straightened. Then he touched his hand to her cheek, tipping her chin upward so that he could gaze into her eyes.

At first Angela worried he'd read every emotion shining from her face. He'd know without a doubt how much she loved him without her saying a word. But she wanted him to hear it from her lips.

"Let me talk first," he said. "I've been waiting to say this since I saw you in Bentiu protesting the treatment of the refugees and women. I've wanted to tell you this since I left you in Chicago all those years ago. I love you more than any man has ever loved any woman. You are the only woman I've ever loved and ever will. I want you to be in my life. If that means giving up the navy, I'll do it. If you want me to follow you all over the world saving one child at a time, I'll do it. The truth is, I can't live without you. I'd take a bullet for you." He laughed and kissed her lips. "I already have. And I'd do it all over again. Please. Please. Please. Tell me you love me. Even if only half as much as I love you. I'll take it. I'll take anything you'll give me."

Angela's heart swelled so much it hurt her chest to breathe. "Now you shush while I talk." She pressed a finger over his lips. "Do I have your attention?"

"Undivided," he said, his lips moving against her finger, sending electrical surges throughout her body.

"When you left me in Chicago, I thought I would die. You were my first love, my only love and hopefully my last love. I can't give my heart to another when you are the one who holds it in your hands." She leaned up on her toes and kissed his lips. "Please don't walk away from me again."

"Darlin', I couldn't do it again. It nearly ripped me apart the first time. If I hadn't gone into the navy and the SEALs, I would have come completely apart. Leaving you was the hardest thing I'd ever done."

"Good. Don't do it again." She touched her hand to his chest. "My heart can't take it a second time."

"Do you want me to get out of the navy?" he asked.

She shook her head. "Not until you're good and ready. Not a day sooner. I can survive the loneliness as long as I know you're coming home to me."

"What if I don't come home?" He gathered her closer. "Or rather, if I come home in a body bag?"

She pulled her bottom lip between her teeth, her heart squeezing hard in her chest. "I'll take whatever time I have with you. If something happens and you don't make it… I'll survive. I know I can live without you. I just prefer not to."

"What are you going to do, now that you're leaving Doctors Without Borders?"

She shrugged. "I thought about going back to the States and back to school to become a surgeon."

Buck grinned. "Liked digging around inside me that much?"

She shook her head. "No. I didn't like not knowing exactly what to do with all the parts and pieces inside. I never want to feel that helpless ever again."

"I hear there are some good medical schools in Virginia."

Angela smiled. "I was thinking the same thing. I could be there when you're home from deployment."

"I'd like that a lot."

"Me, too." She touched a finger to his lips. "Now, you need to eat and rest. I want you to be well and fit the next time we make love."

He waggled his brows. "I'm up to it if you are."

She shook her head. "No way. Not until your stitches are out and you're not in jeopardy of re-opening your wound. I don't want you hurt because of me."

"I'd be willing to risk it."

"Well, I'm not." She took his arm and guided him to the table and the tray of food. "We'll start one step at a time."

"The commander felt bad about interrupting our vacation. We have all week here," Buck said.

Angela laughed. "That's not how I heard it. I heard you were a cranky patient."

He lifted his chin and grinned down at her. "I like to think that I didn't have the right doctor."

"Is that right?" She crossed her arms over her chest. "And who is the right doctor for you?"

"There's only one doctor who can work on my heart. And that's you, babe."

"Lord help me. I don't ever want to have to work on your heart." She touched his chest.

He captured her hand in his. "You have completely captured my heart." Buck pulled her into his arms. "I love you, Dr. Angela Vega, more than life itself. And I promise to always come back to you from wherever I am in the world."

"I love you, Graham Buckner. And I promise to be there, waiting for you."

* * * * *

Get 4 FREE REWARDS!

We'll send you 2 FREE Books
<u>plus</u> 2 FREE Mystery Gifts.

Harlequin® Intrigue books feature heroes and heroines that confront and survive danger while finding themselves irresistibly drawn to one another.

FREE Value Over **$20**

HI18

SPECIAL EXCERPT FROM

(H)HARLEQUIN®

I N T R I G U E

When Annabelle Clementine returns to
Whitehorse, Montana, cowboy Dawson Rogers helps his
ex-girlfriend sell her late grandmother's house to ensure
her swift departure, but first they must solve a mystery...

Read on for a sneak preview of Hard Rustler
by New York Times *bestselling author B.J. Daniels.*

As her sports car topped the rise, Annabelle Clementine looked
out at the rugged country spread before her and felt her heart
drop. She'd never thought she'd see so many miles of wild
winter Montana landscape ever again. At least, she'd hoped not.

How could she have forgotten the remoteness? The vastness?
The isolation? There wasn't a town in sight. Or a ranch house. Or
another living soul.

She glanced down at her gas gauge. It hovered at empty. She'd
tried to get gas at the last station, but her credit card wouldn't
work and she'd gone through almost all of her cash. She'd put in
what fuel she could with the change she was able to scrape up,
but it had barely moved the gauge. If she ran out of gas before she
reached Whitehorse...well, it would just be her luck, wouldn't it?

She let the expensive silver sports car coast down the mountain
toward the deep gorge of the Missouri River, thankful that most
of the snow was high in the mountains and not on the highway.
She didn't know what she would have done if the roads had been
icy since she hadn't seen a snow tire since she'd left Montana.

The motor coughed. She looked down at the gauge. The
engine had to be running on fumes. What was she going to do?
It was still miles to Whitehorse. Tears burned her eyes, but she

refused to cry. Yes, things were bad. Really bad. But—

She was almost to the river bottom when she saw it. At a wide spot where the river wound on its way through Montana east to the Mississippi, a pickup and horse trailer were pulled off to the side of the highway. Her pulse jumped at just the thought of another human being—let alone the possibility of getting some fuel. If she could just get to Whitehorse...

But as she descended the mountain, she didn't see anyone around the pickup or horse trailer. What if the rig had been left beside the road and the driver was nowhere to be found? Maybe there would be a gas can in the back of the pickup or— *Have you stooped so low that now you would steal gas?*

Fortunately, she wasn't forced to answer that. She spotted a cowboy standing on the far side of the truck. Her instant of relief was quickly doused as she looked around and realized how alone the two of them were, out here in the middle of nowhere.

Don't be silly. What are the chances the cowboy is a serial killer, rapist, kidnapper, ax murderer...? The motor sputtered as if taking its last gasp as she slowed. It wasn't as if she had a choice. She hadn't seen another car for over an hour. For miles she'd driven through open country dotted occasionally with cows but no people. And she knew there was nothing but rugged country the rest of the way north to Whitehorse.

If there had been any other way to get where she was headed, she would have taken it. But her options had been limited for some time now.

And today, it seemed, her options had come down to this cowboy and possible serial killer rapist kidnapper ax murderer.

Don't miss Hard Rustler by B.J. Daniels,
available September 2018 wherever
Harlequin® Intrigue books and ebooks are sold.

www.Harlequin.com

HIIEXP0818

*Hawk Cahill let down Deidre "Drey" Hunter
once before. He isn't going to make that mistake again,
especially since she just married the wrong man—a man
who is suddenly missing.*

*Read on for a sneak preview of
RANCHER'S DREAM,
the next book in **THE MONTANA CAHILLS** series
by* New York Times *bestselling author B.J. Daniels.*

You will die in this house.

The thought seemed to rush out of the darkness as the house came into view. The premonition turned her skin clammy. Drey gripped a handful of her wedding dress, her fingers aching but unable to release the expensive fabric as she stared at her new home. A wedding gift, Ethan had said. A surprise, sprung on her at the reception.

The portent still had a death grip on her. She could see herself lying facedown in a pool of water, her auburn hair fanned out around her head, her body so pale it appeared to have been drained of all blood.

"Are you all right?" her husband asked now as he reached over to take her hand. "Dierdre?" Unlike everyone else she knew, Ethan refused to call her by her nickname, Drey

"I'm still a little woozy from the reception," she said, desperately needing fresh air right now as she put down her window to let in the cool Montana summer night.

"I warned you about drinking too much champagne."

He'd warned her about a lot of things. But it wasn't the champagne, which she hadn't touched during the reception. He knew she didn't drink, but he'd insisted one glass of champagne at her wedding wasn't going to kill her. She'd gotten one of the waiters to bring her sparkling cider.

So it wasn't alcohol that had her stomach roiling. No, it was when Ethan told her where they would be living. She'd assumed they would live in his New York City penthouse since that was where he spent most of his time. She'd actually been looking forward to it because she'd grown up in Gilt Edge, Montana, and had never lived in a large city before. Also it would be miles from Gilt Edge—and Hawk Cahill.

She'd never dreamed that Ethan meant for them to live here in Montana, at the place he'd named Mountain Crest. All during construction, she'd thought that the odd structure was to be used as a business retreat only. Ethan had been so proud of the high-tech house with its barred gate at the end of the paved road, she'd never let on that she knew the locals made fun of it—and its builder.

When Ethan had pulled her aside at the reception and told her that they would be living on the mountain overlooking Gilt Edge in his prized house, Dierdre hadn't been able to hide her shock. She'd never dreamed... But then she'd never dreamed she would be married to Ethan Baxter.

Don't miss RANCHER'S DREAM
by B.J. Daniels, available now wherever
Harlequin® books and ebooks are sold.

www.Harlequin.com

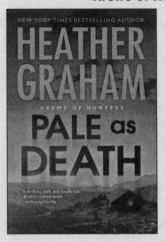